A Touch of Romance

Also available in Large Print
by Anne Hampson:

Destiny

A TOUCH OF ROMANCE

Anne Hampson

G.K.HALL &CO.
Boston, Massachusetts
1989

Published in Large Print by arrangement with
Chivers Press.

G.K. Hall Large Print Book Series.

Set in 16 pt. Plantin.

Library of Congress Cataloging in Publication Data

Hampson, Anne.
    A touch of romance / Anne Hampson.
       p.   cm.—(G.K. Hall large print book series) (Nightingale
series)
    "Published in large print by arrangement with
Chivers Press"—T.p. verso.
   ISBN 0-8161-4879-1 (lg. print)
   1. Large type books. I. Title.
[PR6058.A5547T6   1989]
823' .914—dc20
                                            89-36574

All the characters in this book have no existence outside the imagination of the Author, and have no relation whatsoever to anyone bearing the same name or names. They are not even distantly inspired by any individual known or unknown to the Author, and all the incidents are pure invention.

A Touch of Romance

Chapter One

She had forgiven him twice already, and now he was pleading again, using all his charm and persuasion, trading on the undisputed fact that she still loved him.

Julie stood by the table; she and Mark were in the dining-room of their small detached bungalow, the one they had bought six years ago on their marriage, the 'dear little love nest' into which they had moved so happily on their return from a honeymoon in Spain. It was identical to five others in Oak Tree Close, but in all the others there were children, and Julie often wondered whether, had their little boy lived, they would have remained as close as they were at the beginning.

She stared at him, at the man whose rugged, manly appearance had so quickly set her heart beating overrate, whose smile had seemed to melt the very marrow in her bones.

To be so deeply affected by a man! Unwise—and yet what could one do when one's heart was lost?

The pain in her heart had robbed her face of colour; she felt ten years older than her twenty-five years. And Mark? He seemed to retain his youth no matter what strain or stress assailed him. He was certainly enduring stress at this time, for Julie had just five minutes ago told him she was leaving and that she wanted a divorce.

'I don't believe you!' he had almost snarled. 'You're just trying to frighten me!'

She shook her fair head and looked directly at him.

'There's a limit, Mark. Three times you've been unfaithful—'

'Because you were cold! I'm a normal man; I have my rights. You didn't want me near you, so what do you expect?'

'Understanding,' was her quiet reply. 'When a mother loses her child she can't go on as if nothing has happened.' She stopped, feeling again the excruciating agony she had suffered when she had looked into the face of a police officer and was told her child was dead. Little Roddy would never have been away from home, staying with Mark's mother, if it hadn't been that Mark had insisted on Julie going with him when he was sent to Scotland for three weeks by his firm. It was on the very day they had returned to the bungalow that the accident happened. Roddy had run out on to the road . . .

Mark had actually been on the phone to tell his mother he was coming to collect his son, but there was no reply. So he went off in the car, while Julie busied herself with several jobs at once—the main one of course being the preparation of a meal.

The knock on the door, the uniformed man, tall and sombre-faced—Julie knew she would never forget the sickening lurch of her heart, the swift conviction that Mark had had an accident . . .

It was two years ago and Roddy was just three, a sturdy little boy with fair curly hair, a mischievous gleam in his vivid blue eyes, and a laugh that brought sheer music into the house.

'Understanding!' scoffed Mark balefully. 'You turned from me at a time when we ought to have been comforting one another, and you know it. But you won't admit it—'

'Mark, please don't let's argue,' she

begged in a stifled voice. 'Think whatever you like about me; I don't care.'

'You do care,' he argued harshly. 'You still love me and you always will. And if you do carry out your threat you won't be long in coming back.'

'I shan't come back,' she averred. 'I've had enough, Mark.' She moved over to the window and his eyes followed her. He lit a cigarette, inhaling deeply, and his hand trembled. He could not imagine living here alone, doing everything for himself after coming home to an empty house every time he went out.

'Don't go, darling,' he pleaded. 'Forgive me just this once and I'll never let you down again—I swear it!'

Julie turned, her blue eyes dark with pain.

'You've made promises like that twice before,' she reminded him, and the small sigh of impatience he gave was not lost on her.

'You're unfair in placing all the blame on me, Julie,' he protested, a hint of plaintiveness in his tone. 'As I said, you didn't want me near you. How do you expect a man to live the life of a celibate?'

Bitterness edged her voice as she said, 'So sex is the most important thing that exists between us? What about the love you started off with?'

'I still love you,' Mark stated fiercely, again drawing on his cigarette and inhaling the smoke deep into his lungs. 'You and I will love each other till we die!'

'Then how can you bear to sleep with another woman—three women, in fact?'

'I don't know how you found out about this one,' he complained, turning his back on her as he went for a chair.

'The same as before—I was told.'

'Damned gossips! It's what comes of living in a small place. Everyone makes it their business to spy on others.' Mark lifted the slender dining-chair, then almost threw it down, taking possession of it and tapping his cigarette ash on to the carpet at his feet.

'You can't keep on having affairs and not be found out,' Julie said reasonably. She suddenly saw the woman he'd been with . . . saw in her mind's eye Emma Saunders, whose husband worked abroad for about nine months of every year. Emma was a regular visitor to the local pub, and Julie did not know how Mark could expect his affair with the woman to remain undetected. True, it was winter, so it was always dark when Mark went out—supposedly to

5

play in a darts match—or matches, because they had gone on for weeks. But darkness doesn't always hide everything you want it to, and Mark was seen, more than once, going into Emma's cottage on the other side of the village. When Julie was told by a neighbour, the shock was not nearly as great as on the first occasion. Then it had knocked everything out of her; she had felt her whole world had collapsed and she was being flung deep into an abyss of misery.

It was true she had become cold during those first months after Roddy's death, but she had never dreamed that Mark would find satisfaction elsewhere. She had forgiven him, but somehow it was never the same, and once again, during the weeks following the anniversary of her son's death, she had not wanted Mark to make love to her. But she wanted comfort nevertheless, and this he could not offer on its own.

She looked at him and the love she had once known welled up within her. But at the same time she was wise enough to realise that her marriage was well and truly on the rocks. She could not bear his hands on her because she could see them caressing Emma, the only one of the three whom she had seen. But even before that she had still been able to imagine him caressing those other women. The result was that every moment of his lovemaking was agony for her; she felt dirty, defiled. The beauty had vanished for ever.

'Don't go,' he pleaded again, tossing his cigarette stub into the grate. 'Let's try again, darling. Come to me now; let me kiss your eyes and make them bright with love again.' Rising, he moved swiftly towards her and before she could even think of escaping she was imprisoned in arms as strong as steel.

'Let me go! If you must have lustful satisfaction then go back to her! She's only a mile away—' The rest was stifled by his hungry mouth; he devoured hers in spite of her struggles. His hands roamed; her bodice was torn in his anger and she cried out at the ruthless way he gripped her breast. Lifting her, he carried her, struggling, to the bedroom. Once there, he took hold of the neck of her blouse at the back and one sharp sweep brought it away. Julie stood there quivering with rage, hot colour washing into her face, her heart pounding with sickening force against her ribcage. 'I won't let you make love to me,' she began, but he interrupted her harshly.

'You'll give me my rights—willingly or

the other way! Do you get those clothes off or would you like me to do it for you?'

She looked at the door, ajar . . .

'There's no escape, Julie.' His voice was quieter but the harshness was still there. 'Well, are you getting undressed?'

For answer she made a grab for her dressing-gown which was lying neatly on the end of the bed. Mark snatched it from her and the next moment, fury breaking, he almost tore her clothes from her trembling body. Naked at last, she stood there, resigned, and watched him unbutton his shirt.

When presently his hands were exploring ruthlessly she lay very still and silent, but she knew her attitude would only increase her husband's fury, and she was very soon the victim of a primitive passion he had never exhibited with her before. His hands were cruel on her breasts, his fingers tightening on her nipples with calculated slow torture until her eyes were filled with tears. And when at last he took her it was more in hate than love—in fact, in that moment Julie was awakened to the fact that, whatever love he had had for her in the beginning, it was now dead.

Julie smiled at her flatmate and said yes,

she looked most attractive, at which Angela laughed and said with a twinkle in her hazel eyes, 'You think I'm vain, so why not say so?'

'You're vain, Angela.'

'Cat!'

Julie shrugged and sat down on the couch, crossing her slender legs one over the other. Angela looked at her for a long moment and then, a curious inflection in her voice, 'Why aren't you coming with me to the party? You were invited; I heard Elaine asking you to come.'

'I've got some sewing to do. I want to shorten that dress I bought on Saturday.'

'It can keep. There's no urgency, seeing it's for your holidays. You don't go till late September and it's only July now.'

'I'm not in a party mood, Angela.' Again Julie smiled, noting the way the pretty nylon and lace dress fitted snugly to her friend's breasts and waist. Peach suited her dark hair and the pearl eardrops seemed just right. 'Don't worry about me. I'm happy to be staying in—honestly I am.'

'You don't talk much about yourself, do you?' said Angela curiously.

'There isn't much to tell.'

'I rather think that's one big fib and there's a lot to tell!'

'Well, I'm not a confiding person and you know it already.'

'Okay—but I'll bet you'll open up one day, and if you do, pet, you'll have a sympathetic ear.' And with that Angela tripped to the chair, picked up her evening bag and went out. Julie heard her in the tiny square hall and judged she was putting on a coat. The door opened, then banged, and Julie was alone in the two-bedroomed flat she had come to seven months ago when, the morning after that never-to-be-forgotten night with her impassioned husband, she had packed all her clothes and walked out of the bungalow into the waiting taxi.

She had seen the advertisement two weeks previously: 'Business girl wishes for similar to share her flat in Bournemouth.' Julie had rung the number given, had liked the voice which had answered, and a meeting had been arranged. But at this time Julie had not quite made up her mind. She still loved her husband, and no matter what he had done she knew it would tear her apart to leave him. Yet on the other hand she was vitally aware of the change in herself, the reluctance to give herself because always she would imagine him making love to the other women. Forgiveness must be complete if the marriage is to survive, she had told herself.

But Julie could neither forgive nor forget. The first time, yes, she did forgive him completely, but try as she would, she could not forget.

She had told Angela she would let her know, and this she had done, but saying she could not give the exact date when she would move into the flat. Julie had intended moving a few days later than she did, but after that night she was not taking any more chances; she had no intention of leaving herself open to that kind of bestial treatment ever again. And so she had phoned Angela early, catching her before she went to work—and phoning while Mark was taking his shower. If Angela thought there was anything strange about Julie's ringing at this hour, and also wanting to move into the flat right away, she said nothing. She had taken to Julie on sight, soon realising that there was something amiss in her life, but at that time she curbed her curiosity, for after all, Julie was as yet a complete stranger. However, as the weeks and months went by, Angela quite naturally became more and more curious. She had tried once or twice, by subtle questions, to draw Julie out, but without success. Julie was friendly by nature and pleasant to live with, so Angela endeavoured to contain her curiosity, albeit with, at times, the greatest of difficulty.

Julie had been fortunate in landing a job in the same firm as Angela.

'There's a secretary's job going,' she had told Julie one evening when she came home. 'You were saying you wanted a job and that you'd had secretarial training, so why don't you apply for it?'

And without difficulty Julie had got the job, and was very happy in it, her boss being the placid type and also old enough to be taking life easy.

But there was a certain restlessness within Julie which she was unable to combat, or even completely to understand. There was no doubt in her mind that she had done the right thing in leaving her husband, and although in a way she still loved him, she never contemplated the possibility of going back. If, at the age of thirty, he had already been unfaithful to her three times, how many more times would he have been unfaithful to her?

She fetched the dress from her wardrobe,

but somehow she could not concentrate and she put it back without even having done one stitch. Perhaps she should have gone to Elaine's party with Angela. Elaine was chief designer in the firm of Copeland (Kathleen) Limited, dress manufacturers. The firm had factories in several industrial towns, but the offices were in Bournemouth, and there was also a small factory where all the designing was done and the samples made up. No bulk manufacturing took place here; it was merely the hub of a very large and prosperous wheel, and most women knew that the label 'Kathleen' meant both good design and quality. Mr Copeland was the Managing Director, and it was for him that Angela worked as private secretary. Mr Holding, Julie's boss, looked after the export side of the business, but it was the man under him who did most of the work, so this meant that Julie quite often found herself with nothing much to do, and on more than one occasion Mr Holding had said casually, his pale blue eyes tired beneath bushy grey eyebrows, 'You might as well take the day off tomorrow, Miss Bennett—and the next day you needn't come in until after lunch.'

Miss Bennett . . . Julie had resumed her maiden name, though she had had to explain to Mr Holding that she was married. Her private life was her own, he had commented carelessly, so she had no difficulty in dropping Mark's name.

She often wondered if he had tried to find her, but felt she had covered her tracks so well that he would not succeed even if he did try. Some day soon she would see a solicitor about a divorce. Best to get it all over and done with so that Mark could marry again if he wished.

Still restless, Julie decided to go to bed with a book and hope that sleep would not be too long coming to her. Reading in bed did usually make her eyes droop after half an hour or so . . .

It was a week later that Mr Holding called her into his office and asked her to sit down.

'No, don't bother opening your notebook—' He waved a hand negligently and Julie closed the book, sending him a puzzled glance.

'We've got a client—no, a potential client,' he corrected, 'in Greece—Athens. He's coming over in about two weeks' time to see some of our samples. He wants them modelled.' A slight pause as he let his eyes rove over Julie's figure. 'We've decided that, for the small sizes of most of the dresses, we shall use you—'

'M-me!' exclaimed Julie, going hot about the collar. 'I can't model, Mr Holding!'

He smiled faintly.

'Have you ever tried, Miss Bennett?' he enquired, and she shook her head. 'You know, someone once asked Winston Churchill if he could play a violin. His reply was that he didn't know as he'd never tried.'

Julie had to laugh. But she was instantly serious again as she said, 'I'd make a mess of it, Mr Holding. One needs training to be a model.'

'A professional model, yes, of course one requires training. But we're not asking you to be a professional, or expecting miracles. You'll just parade before this Mr—Mr—' He glanced down then flicked a paper over and then another, 'Mr Dardanis—Christos Dardanis. He's an entrepreneur—the largest women's clothing wholesaler in Greece. He sells only quality clothes, branded names. From what I've heard about him from Mr Portman, who as you know works under me and does a great deal of negotiating with foreign buyers, this Mr Dardanis is extremely particular; he'll turn the samples inside out. If we can get his custom it will mean one of the biggest deals we've ever had. He's expressed the wish to see the samples worn—'

'I'm sorry, Mr Holding,' Julie broke in agitatedly, 'but I just couldn't parade in front of this man!'

'My dear girl,' sighed her boss exasperatedly, 'there's no need for panic. The man won't eat you. All you're being asked to do is wear the dresses, skirts and blouses, walk in front of him and then go off and change into something else. He'll probably be tired of the whole performance in ten minutes or so.'

'From what you've said, Mr Holding, I don't think he'll get tired until he's seen the whole range—and it would take hours to model them all.'

'Stand up,' he said, ignoring this observation. 'Yes, as Mr Copeland says, your figure is perfect.'

'Mr—!' She stared at him. The austere Mr Copeland taking notice of one of his office girls! 'You mean he—he . . .' Her voice trailed off and she felt the hot colour fuse her cheeks.

'Yes, he's noticed your figure,' he almost snapped. 'All men look twice at a figure like yours, Miss Bennett. You must be aware of your attractions—I've never yet met a woman who isn't.'

Julie felt herself getting even hotter. She knew she had a passable figure, but—perfect . . . And from none other than the great Mr Copeland himself!

'As I said,' she began, with the intention of making an even firmer protest this time, but she was instantly interrupted not only by an impatient wave of her boss's hand, but by the opening of the office door. Mr Copeland came in and his eyes ran over her from head to foot.

'You've obviously been told by Mr Holding what we want of you,' he said, and automatically she nodded, suddenly thinking that up till now her job had been rather too easy. She was now expected to do something in addition to her secretarial duties, and in all fairness she had to admit that she ought not to be objecting at all. But it was such a *different* job! She'd feel such a fool, parading up and down trying to look as if she were an accomplished model. She said, in response to Mr Copeland's words, 'I have, sir, but surely an experienced model would sell our dresses far better than I would?'

'It's merely a matter of someone wearing the clothes for this potential customer to see,' rejoined Mr Copeland casually. 'No, we shan't be requiring any models. You will manage the small sizes and Miss Forbes and Miss Townsend the others. Well, you ought to be feeling flattered, Miss Bennett,' he went on briskly. He looked at his colleague. 'When is this man coming over?'

'He didn't give a definite date, merely saying he'd be here within the next two weeks but would let us know the date by Friday.'

Mr Copeland was nodding absently and after a moment he had left the office.

Julie was dismissed, and she went without further argument. She didn't want to get herself the sack.

'Angela, I feel such a fool!'

'Rubbish! You're great. Walk over there again.' Angela was seated on a low stool, eating an apple, while Julie was walking about, head held high, shoulders back. She said again, 'I feel like a fool!'

'I think you ought to take up modelling. You're doing fine.'

'Why does the wretched man want to see someone wearing the clothes anyway?' sighed Julie. 'Other customers are quite satisfied with being *shown* the samples!'

'He's fastidious, from what I've been hearing. Fussy! I guess he's ancient—a grizzled old Greek with millions of lines on his face and a bent back.'

Julie stopped walking and laughed heartily.

'I won't be able to keep a straight face if he does turn out to fit your picture!'

'Greeks are stocky and have gold fillings; they twirl worry beads all the time—though what they have to worry about heaven only knows! Their wives do all the work!'

'He's a darned nuisance! I'll be so hot and bothered, parading in front of him,' complained Julie.

'Ignore him and just walk. Pretend he isn't there.'

'Easier said than done.' Julie walked across the room again, wishing one wall were a mirror so she could see herself. 'I only hope he's so old that he can't stand it for more than a few minutes.'

'He'll be old, all right,' said Angela. 'Greek men get old before they're thirty because of all the sex they indulge in. Sexiest men in the world—that's the reputation the Greeks have.'

Julie looked at her.

'You seem to know a good deal about them,' she observed.

'I've been to Greece on holiday—twice. The men mentally strip you all the time—' Angela stopped abruptly as her friend swung around.

'Thanks for the information! I feel much better now!'

'Oh . . .' Angela clapped a hand to her mouth, but her eyes betrayed that she was giggling. 'I'm an idiot—sorry!' She gave a sudden shrug of her shoulders. 'He'll be past it, love, so forget what I said.'

Julie glared at her, then laughed ruefully.

'I sincerely hope you're right, Angela, and that he's too old and decrepit to be interested in my anatomy!'

Chapter Two

Ignore him, Angela had advised. Pretend he isn't there.

Julie had been fully expecting the Greek to be old, and now she could not help wondering why both she and Angela had come to that sort of conclusion. She stood now, seconds after Mr Copeland had said by way of introduction, 'This young lady, Miss

Bennett, will be wearing the samples, Mr Dardanis—that is, the smaller sizes.'

Julie just stood there, mesmerised by the unusual height of the man, for he must be six feet two at least; and his features . . . Finely chiselled and classical, they alone gave him an air of distinction which Julie had never seen in a man before. His perfect physique, with those erect broad shoulders, that narrow waist and those slender hips. Yet through the fine grey linen of his slacks was the idea of sinewed strength, and this was patent in the hands as well—long slender hands giving a very false impression unless one used one's imagination, which Julie somehow found herself doing, and reaching the conclusion that those hands could be as strong as vices if the occasion required it. His hair was raven black, his eyes tawny brown, deep-set and piercing below straight black, well-defined brows. His cheekbones, prominent above hollowed cheeks, provided further evidence of his noble ancestry—in fact, thought Julie, he might be a god himself! Yes, a god of ancient Greece—but of course he was wearing the wrong clothes. His skin, very brown, suggested an outdoor life as much as inheritance. He regarded her unsmilingly, but when he spoke to Mr Copeland strong, per-fect white teeth were revealed.

Julie felt worse than ever about the task she was to perform. In fact, she had to exercise the greatest control not to feign illness, or think of some other excuse in order to escape.

'Perhaps the young lady will wear, first, the princess dress and then the pink taffeta ball dress.' Christos Dardanis's voice was low and finely-timbred and carrying the hint of an accent which added to the attractive-ness of the tone.

'Go on, Miss Bennett.' Mr Copeland was sitting now, next to the Greek, with Mr Holding a few feet away. Elaine, looking rather anxious, was standing to one side of the large conference room in which the 'fashion show' was being held. All the de-signs were hers, so Julie could well under-stand how anxious she must be.

Making a tremendous effort to still her trembling, Julie came forward and walked past the three men without looking at any of them. Then she stopped and of course had to glance up then. The Greek's eyes met hers, then they roved over her entire body, resting for a fleeting space first on her breasts, then her waist and, lastly, on her hips. A flood of heat washed over her, for she felt she had indeed been stripped of every shred of cover. She brought her long lashes down, unaware of the delectable shadows they cast on to her hot cheeks.

'You can go and change.' It was Christos Dardanis who issued the order, in a quiet yet imperious tone of voice. Julie went swiftly, every nerve affected by the undisguised sensuality of the man's examination of her body.

The ball dress was in pale rose silk taffeta, a really stunning creation with off-the-shoulder flounced sleeves and a full tiered skirt trimmed with tiny silk roses. The bodice was far tighter than Julie would have wished, yet the dress was her size for all that. It was meant to be tight, to hug the curves and accentuate them. From somewhere Mr Copeland had produced a choker to wear with it, a pale grey choker made of freshwater pearls. Julie wore no earrings, but on her left wrist was a bracelet that matched the choker. She felt like a million dollars and could actually have enjoyed wearing this lovely gown had it been in different circumstances. As it was, she began to tremble all over again as she walked back into the room, to parade herself once again before the three men. She caught Elaine's eyes and a smile fluttered. Elaine responded, and neither noticed the odd expression that had fleetingly crossed the foreigner's face when Julie gave Elaine that smile.

'Turn around.' The order came in an abrupt voice, and Julie obeyed, feeling rather what she imagined a slave of old would have felt like, awaiting the approval of a purchaser. The comparison brought an involuntary smile of humour to her lips, and as she was turning again by this time all three men noticed the smile, but it was the Greek who commented on it, asking with a lift of his arrogant brows, 'What is so amusing, Miss Bennett?' and of course this unexpected question naturally set her out of countenance—as the man probably hoped it would, she suddenly realised, and her chin lifted at the same time as a sparkle entered her eyes.

'I was laughing at some secret thought, sir. Er—can I go now?'

The tawny eyes glinted and the sensuous mouth tightened.

'Not yet. Turn around again.'

Julie bit her lip as she again obeyed. He was deliberately making her feel small and inferior. She felt she hated him—yes, with a black venom!

'Walk over there.'

She turned around.

'Where?' she asked, avoiding the stares of the two other men.

Christos Dardanis flung out an imperious hand.

'Walk up and down the room—No, that way first.'

Gritting her teeth, Julie once more did as she was told. 'And again.'

She hesitated, glancing at Mr Copeland. He nodded urgently and frowned at the same time.

Julie paraded herself, feeling that if that hateful man asked her once more she would march out of the room even if it did mean losing her job! However, he waved her away and said. 'The ivory evening dress next, please.'

Please . . . I'll bet that was a strain! Julie said to herself as she thankfully left the room.

Puffed sleeves and lace panels were the focus points of the ivory taffeta evening dress, which fitted Julie to perfection, as both of the others had done. The bodice was again tight-fitting, the neckline scooped and rather too revealing for Julie's taste. The Greek's eyes seemed to glitter as they rested on her breasts, and again she flushed. To her chagrin she saw the fine lips twitch and realised her heightened colour had amused him. Hateful creature!

There had been no comment on the dresses up till now, and the mask-like expression of the Greek gave nothing away. Suppose it was all a waste of time and he decided not to buy anything?

Suddenly Julie felt troubled, and she mentioned her concern to Elaine while she was changing into a midnight blue cocktail dress.

'It can't be helped if he doesn't buy anything, so don't look so concerned.' Elaine was dealing with tiny pearl buttons at the back of the dress.

'But it's you I'm thinking about, Elaine. All you've put into these designs, and they're beautiful.'

'The man's an odd bod if ever there was one,' said Elaine. 'Not a muscle in his face moves when he's looking at the dresses, not the hint of a change of expression to tell us whether or not he likes what we're offering.'

'I think he's hateful!'

'That's strong, but I do understand your

feelings,' the older girl commiserated. 'He was downright rude with you. I should ask for a rise after this ordeal!'

'I wish it were over. Angela didn't think he'd stick it out very long and neither did Mr Holding,' said Julie.

But Christos Dardanis sat there for over two hours, and never once did he speak other than to order Julie to do this or that. She sent him glowering looks, uncaring as time dragged on that he might decide not to buy anything. To the devil with him! The sooner he took himself back to Greece the better.

It was three days later, and Julie was again called into Mr Holding's office.

Christos Dardanis was sitting there, leaning carelessly against the back of the chair and with one arm resting loosely on the cushioned support at his elbow. His long legs were crossed one over the other, his immaculate dark blue slacks hitched up to reveal very short socks and an inch or so of bronzed leg above them.

The nonchalant pose seemed to irritate Julie for no reason she could explain. She supposed she just disliked the man so much that everything about him annoyed her.

'Ah, Miss Bennett!' Mr Holding was fairly beaming at her as she came forward to stand in front of his desk. The Greek was to her left and she was vitally aware of his intense scrutiny, but she determinedly avoided meeting those searching and—she suspected—critical eyes.

Critical . . . Mr Holding's next words gave the lie to this idea and at the same time stunned Julie into a stupefied silence of disbelief.

'You'll be pleased to know that Mr Dardanis has given us a very large order—on condition that you go over to Greece to model for him. We are of course happy to loan you to him for an indefinite period.' He leant back, rubbed his chubby hands and waited expectantly for Julie to speak. But she was dumb. It was the Greek who presently broke the silence, to say with a sort of mocking amusement, 'The idea does not seem to meet with your approval, Miss Bennett?' She glared at him, unable to think of a worse fate than to have him as a boss.

'I'm sure, Mr Dardanis,' she said coldly, 'that you would fare much better with an experienced model.'

'So you are not willing to model these clothes?'

She shook her head.

'I am not, Mr Dardanis,' she returned emphatically.

'Miss Bennett! You don't know what you're saying!' Mr Holding leant forward and frowned at her. 'Firstly, it's the chance of a lifetime, and secondly, Mr Dardanis will not give us the order unless you're willing to model for him.'

Julie's blue eyes kindled. She was not likely to forget those sensuous and often prolonged examinations of her body, as the time dragged on. And what had Angela said about the Greeks? They're the sexiest men in the world.

She looked squarely at her boss and said, 'I'm very sorry, Mr Holding, but I'm not willing to go with this m— with Mr Dardanis to Greece.'

'But why?' he asked angrily, seeing the massive order slip away through the stubbornness of this stupid girl. 'It's not as if you've got any ties here. You told me you share a flat with Angela—'

'Forget it,' broke in Christos Dardanis, rising from his chair and lifting a lean brown hand to stifle a yawn. 'As there's nothing more to say, I'll bid you good day.' He went to the door, walking with a sort of majestic hauteur that at once set Julie's hackles rising. Was ever a man as arrogant and full of his own conceit as this foreigner!

'Just a moment, Mr Dardanis!' cried Mr Holding. 'Please don't go yet. This matter can be resolved . . .' His voice trailed as the door closed quietly behind the Greek. He glowered at his secretary and said explosively, 'Do you realise what you've done? You've lost this firm the largest order they've ever had!'

'It isn't any fault of mine,' she protested, fully convinced that she would get her notice within the next hour. 'I didn't want to model the dresses in the first place. Why should I go to Greece when I don't want to?' She felt miserable, for although she was vehemently maintaining that she was blameless, she was, for all that, feeling guilty because of the loss of such a big order.

'I don't know what Mr Copeland will say: we've already been congratulating ourselves—' Mr Holding broke off and sagged in his chair. 'You may go, Miss Bennett,' he added after a space. 'Needless to say, I'm disgusted with your refusal to help your employers. I'm very disappointed in you indeed.'

Elaine shook her head and sat down dejectedly. Julie, amazed that she had not received her notice even though it was now the day following her refusal to go to Greece, stared at the girl who had just told her that, because of the loss of that order, one of the factories would have to go on short time. Julie and Elaine and Angela had had lunch in the staff canteen and Elaine had not spoken more than half a dozen words.

When lunch was over she had asked Julie to go with her into the cutting-room, and it was here that she had imparted the bad news.

'We've been hit like everyone else these days,' she went on unhappily, 'but we knew that if this Greek did place an order with us, and we carried it out to his satisfaction, we'd be able to rely on his custom indefinitely. And as he sells throughout Greece and several other countries, we could have kept all our machinists busy—' She broke off and gave a resigned shrug of her shoulders. 'But why am I telling you all this, Julie? I don't altogether blame you for not wanting to go to a strange country.'

Julie knew full well that Elaine did blame her—that everyone blamed her. She had been offered a substantial rise in salary if

31

she would change her mind, but still she had refused. She felt trapped, then angry that this should be so. It wasn't fair of anyone to blame her for the loss of the order. And most certainly it wasn't fair of the Greek to make a condition like that.

Suddenly Julie was suspicious of his motives again. Surely he wanted to give the order, otherwise he would never have offered at all. He really wanted the merchandise, and yet he would let it go unless Julie went along with it.

'It doesn't make sense,' she was telling Angela that evening over their meal. 'That man has some ulterior motive!'

'Could have.' Angela, while understanding how Julie felt, was at the same time a little surprised that she hadn't at least given the matter more consideration. The rise in salary for one thing—that would have been enough to tempt Angela. Then there was the interesting change of occupation from secretary to model, and not by any means least was the travel, the novelty of living in another country for a while. She said tentatively at last, 'It wouldn't be for ever, you know.'

Julie, pale but resolved, said shortly, 'You

blame me as well, don't you, Angela—for the girls having to go on short time?'

'You've every right to please yourself,' was the evasive reply, and Julie changed the subject.

Later, Angela went out for the evening, and once again Julie got out her dress with the intention of shortening it. But as before she was restless, and this time she did know the reason, of course. Why couldn't her life run smoothly, like most of the people she knew? Well, at least she was fast recovering from the traumatic experience of the break-up of her marriage, and she had lately realised that the pain of loving Mark was disappearing far more quickly than she would ever have believed. She felt nothing these days—except relief that she didn't have to sleep with him. That last night had put her off sex for good, she told herself.

Again she put the dress away, and, instead of the sewing she played records for over two hours. She made herself coffee, then spent half an hour reading a book. At a quarter to eleven she yawned and stretched and decided it was time for bed. A shower would be nice . . .

She was in a dainty see-through nightie and matching négligé when the bell rang.

Angela had obviously left her key behind. Julie went to the door just as she was, a smile on her lips which froze immediately she opened the door.

'You—!' She pushed the door quickly, but Mark had his foot in it, and as his strength was greater than hers he was inside in seconds and had slammed the door behind him.

'Yes, I found you,' he gritted, and she realised he had been drinking. 'Don't ask me how, because I shan't tell you, but I discovered you'd taken a flat here—'

'It isn't mine,' she broke in urgently, and at the same time stepping backwards, groping for the little hallstand, so as to avoid bumping into it. 'The flat belongs to someone else. She lives here.'

'Don't give me that!' he snarled. 'Are you trying to say you share it?'

'I do share it.' Fear rising within her made her voice take on a husky note. 'She'll be back in a few minutes.'

Mark laughed, a harsh laugh that grated on Julie's ears.

'Trying to scare me off, eh? Well, it's no go! I'm here to claim my rights—' His eyes, insolent for the very first time, raked her body from head to foot. 'All ready and smelling nice. You still use the same bath perfume—very tempting and sexy—' He reached out; she turned and ran into the sitting-room, her heart thundering against her ribs: she felt almost physically sick with fear. How had Mark found her? He gripped her wrist, twisting it brutally, and jerked her trembling body to him. His mouth was closing down on hers even though she continued to struggle, twisting this way and that, getting bruised as his fingers bit into her flesh.

She was just about at the end of her strength by the time his mouth touched hers, his breath sickening her, when the sound she had been waiting for—*praying* for—was heard by them both.

Mark's hold on her body relaxed.

'What the hell's that?' he demanded, voice now slurring.

'Angela!' screamed Julie, almost hysterical. 'Thank God you're here!' Released as her husband swung around, she almost collapsed on to the floor at his feet. But she did manage to totter to a chair and sink into it, forehead and palms damp and with every nerve in her body rioting. Every vestige of colour was washed from her face and her lips were moving convulsively when Angela came into the room.

'Who the devil are you?' demanded Mark belligerently before she could utter a word.

'Angela,' managed Julie tremulously, 'this is my husband. He's attacked m-me—oh, thank God you arrived when you did!' she cried again, and a fit of uncontrolled weeping shook her entire frame.

Angela's eyes flickered from one to the other before she said, holding wide the door, 'Out! You're trespassing in my home. Get out before I phone the police.'

'Why, you—! All right, but I take my wife with me—' Mark turned and made a grab at Julie's scanty clothing, dragging her to her feet. Angela, fury in her eyes, ran at once to her friend's rescue and, taking off her shoe, hit him over the head with it. A guttural cry of pain echoed through the room and at the same time he released his wife, but with a shove that sent her reeling back against the table. Angela eyed Mark challengingly.

'Are you going, or do you want some more?'

For a long moment there was silence: Julie, looking at him swaying there, much the worse for drink and with a hand to his injured head, wondered what she had ever seen in him.

She said huskily, 'Please go, Mark, and don't ever come back.'

He swung around, face twisting convulsively.

'I'll go, yes—but as for not coming back— I'll be back, and you, wife, will pack your things and come away with me, back to where you belong, understand?' White to the lips, and with her hands behind her back gripping the edge of the table for support, Julie nevertheless had the courage to say defiantly, 'Our marriage is over, Mark, finished for good! You won't come here again, remember?'

'I shall come, again and again, until you come home! I'll never give you a moment's peace! And if you leave here and go somewhere else, I'll still find you. You're my wife, and you won't desert me! I shan't let you—'

'Get out!' from Angela threateningly. 'If you're not outside that front door in ten seconds I'll telephone the police and have you arrested for illegal entry into my home!'

Gritting his teeth, he turned to glower at her, but to Julie's great relief he had the sense to go. At the door he turned.

'Remember what I've said, Julie. I shall find you wherever you go!' And with that he lurched forward, almost crashing into Angela but narrowly missing her by inches, and the next moment the two girls were alone in the flat.

'Thank you,' quivered Julie, and started to cry again. 'It—w-was awful!'

'I'll make some tea,' decided Angela practically as she discarded her coat and threw it over the back of a chair. 'You needn't talk if you don't want to, but I'd be a good listener if you do.'

Half an hour later they were going to bed and Julie had told her friend everything. Angela seemed on the point of saying something, but whatever it was she decided it would keep, at least till the morning.

'You've had a tough time,' she said after they had both risen from their chairs. She had the tea tray in her hands and she was looking at Julie, angrily noting the disordered hair, the swollen eyes, the clenched fists at her sides.

'He wasn't like that before,' Julie said huskily. 'He only took to drink after he'd had an—an affair with the first girl—Angela, do you think it's I who am to blame?'

'Not at all,' in a taut and emphatic voice.

'A husband is there to comfort his wife at times like that—or he should be. Your husband seems utterly selfish to me, and I guess the marriage went right only while everything in his life was running smoothly. Did he suppose it would run smoothly till he died?' Angela's voice was thick with contempt. 'We all have ups and downs, and it's when the downs come along that a married couple need each other most. If you want my frank opinion, Julie, your husband's a swine and you're far better off without him.'

The following morning at breakfast Julie said, 'I'll have to leave here, Angela. You do understand, don't you?'

Silence; Angela refilled both their coffee cups.

'I believe he'll find you wherever you are . . . in this country,' she said at last, and the measured significance of her words were only a complement to what Julie had been seriously thinking about as she lay awake for hours before sleep claimed her. She looked at her friend across the table and said reluctantly, 'I ought to accept the offer to go to Greece—that's what you're really saying?'

Angela nodded.

'And you've already been considering it,

apparently.' She passed the sugar and Julie absently picked up two lumps.

'I hate that Greek!' she cried. 'You didn't see how he treated me, but Elaine did. He was a brute!'

Her friend smiled faintly.

'That's a bit of an exaggeration—it must be. However, he's a businessman through and through, from what I've heard, so any abruptness will be just his way—'

'He was more than abrupt. I wouldn't have minded that.'

'Then what was he like?' asked Angela curiously.

'Bossy, and arrogant and superior. He treated me like dirt.'

Angela gave a small sigh.

'I feel, though, that you really ought to consider accepting his offer. You'll still be working for Copelands, remember: you'll only be on loan.'

'That man has some ulterior motive—' Julie began.

'Nonsense, Julie. You've gone off all men because of Mark's conduct, but that'll pass. Go to Greece and get out of Mark's way. Start divorce proceedings and get rid of him once and for all—'

'I have a terrible fear, Angela, that he'll

pester me for the rest of my life,' Julie confessed worriedly.

'Not once you're divorced, but I agree he'll continue to pester you meanwhile, so it's all the more reason for your getting out of the country.' Angela looked at her straight. 'If it were me, Julie,' she continued after a pause, 'I'd take this opportunity of getting out of the country as a heaven-sent chance of escape.'

Julie toyed with a piece of toast, not at all surprised that she wasn't hungry. That arrogant Greek! To have to work for him, obey all those snapped out orders . . .

It was unthinkable . . . but it was also unthinkable that she should be vulnerable to her husband's drunken attacks. She shuddered at the picture of what would have happened if Angela had not made her timely appearance.

'I suppose,' she murmured almost to herself at last, 'that the Greek is the lesser of two evils.'

Angela curbed the laughter that leapt to her lips. But she did say with a hint of amusement, 'I wonder what the conceited Mr Dardanis would say if he could hear himself described as the lesser of two evils!'

She paused a moment and then, fixing Julie's gaze, 'You'll go to Greece, then?'

Julie's hesitancy did not last more than a few seconds.

'Yes,' she said, but with a deep, deep sigh on her lips, 'I'll go.'

'Let's hope it isn't too late,' mused Angela as the thought occurred to her.

'If it is, and he's returned to Greece already, then it's fate that I haven't got to go.'

'I rather think,' Angela returned with sudden conviction, 'that it's fate that you *will* go to Greece with him.'

Chapter Three

Julie sat by the window in her first class seat and tried to concentrate on an article about Bangkok in the in-flight magazine. The man beside her was absorbed in the *Guardian* and she sent him a surreptitious, oblique glance, affected in spite of herself by his clear-cut, attractive profile. She noticed his extraordinarily long lashes, his high, fleshless cheekbones, and the proud way his head was set on wide, powerful shoulders. She wondered, not for the first time, if he was married, and could not make up her mind. Although he had the maturity of a much older man she had guessed his age at no more than twenty-seven or eight. His sheer self-confidence belonged not only to a man of maturity but also to a man of the world.

At one moment, while they were sitting in the first class lounge waiting to board the plane, she had felt a little shock of surprise that she was glad he wasn't the old man which she and Angela had expected—nor was he even middle-aged. He was still young, and the knowledge had, for some indefinable reason, been pleasant.

He turned now, as if sensing her deep interest, and as their eyes met she felt the colour rise to her cheeks. Yet somehow she could not turn away, but waited instead for him to speak.

'What's the matter? Can't you concentrate?' he asked.

'I haven't flown before,' was all she offered in response to this.

'But that's not what is worrying you.' A statement rather than a question, and she answered after a small pause.

'It's a big step to take—leaving one's country to work abroad.'

The trace of a smile momentarily softened the austerity of his dark, Greek features.

'People are doing it all the time.' His eyes flickered over her face. 'You sound like a girl up from the country.' The accented voice was faintly clipped, and it was curious. Folding his newspaper, he slipped it into the rack in front of him. 'Tell me something about yourself,' he invited, and Julie felt her nerves tense, for this was a question she had dreaded. There was a long hesitation before she said,

'There isn't much to tell. My parents died in a car accident when I was seventeen.' She paused, thinking of that tragic period in her life. Mark had come along eighteen months later and within six months they were married. Nineteen was far too young, an aged aunt who had since died warned her, and she did wonder if, had her parents lived, she would have rushed into marriage so quickly, and at such an early age. 'I've been sharing a flat with a friend,' she went on hurriedly, realising her companion was waiting for her to continue. 'She works at the same place as I do—at Copelands.'

'You've never had a steady boy-friend?' Something in the way he said that made her feel alert in a way she could not quite fathom.

That he was keenly interested in her reply was more than evident.

She shook her head after the merest pause. Her private life had nothing to do with him, she decided. He ought not to be questioning her anyway.

'No, I haven't gone—steady with any-one.' She felt herself go hot and tense at the lie. She wondered if he had noticed the hesitation and felt sure he was perceptive enough to have done so. Perhaps he believed she was lying—well, let him! She said, to change the subject, 'How long am I to be with you, Mr Dardanis?'

'I can't give you an answer to that just yet. I want to hold several fashion shows—'

'I'm not a trained model—you know that.'

'Please don't interrupt me,' he snapped. 'One of the first things my employees learn is to respect me.'

Julie bit her lip in anger.

'I'm still employed by Copelands,' she reminded him.

'On loan to me. This means that while you are with me, and receiving your salary from me, you will give me the normal respect due to your employer.'

She lapsed into silence after that, and he took out his newspaper again. But about half an hour before they were due to land she asked a little anxiously, 'This apartment in Athens you told me about—shall I be living there alone?'

He turned to her.

'The apartment is mine. I have a resident housekeeper, so you have nothing to worry about—'

'You mean,' she broke in quiveringly, 'I'm to live with you—er—I mean, in your flat?'

'It's a large one,' he said, and stifled a yawn as if he was bored with the subject. Nevertheless, Julie could not help but pursue it.

'I'd much rather have an apartment of my own, Mr Dardanis—if you don't mind.'

'I do mind,' with suave imperiousness. 'There's a very good reason why I require you to live in my flat.'

Tensed, she sat upright, her hands clenched. She had not fully trusted this man before, but now she was even more suspicious of his motives in bringing her here.

'Will you explain further, Mr Dardanis?' she quivered.

'You'll call me Christos from now on,' was his brusque order, and she gasped in disbelief.

'I can't do that—!'

'I hope you will . . . Julie.' His tone had changed dramatically; he was no longer the stern and arrogant employer, and to Julie the change was both staggering and profoundly disturbing. She felt herself balanced on a knife-edge and bewildered that she could not explain why this strange sensation assailed her.

'Mr Dardanis,' she began in a voice edged with trepidation, 'there's something I don't understand. I feel—feel—like going back . . .' Her voice trailed to silence as she pictured returning to the flat—But no, she would have to uproot herself and find somewhere else, where she could stay—in fear—until Mark found her, and then she would have to uproot herself all over again. And as she had hinted to Angela, she felt that Mark would never cease pursuing her even when the divorce was through. No, she could not go back, yet she did not want to go forward, not with this Greek who without doubt had some scheme in mind, a scheme in which she was to be deeply involved. What must she do?

'You won't go back,' he said with such confidence in his accented voice that, startled, she shot a glance at his profile. It was almost as if he knew every single thing about her! 'There's no need for this panic,' he went on with some asperity. 'I shan't eat you.'

'You haven't explained,' Julie reminded him, resolved to appear calmer since she did not at all like his use of the word, 'panic'. 'I think you will agree, Mr Dardanis, that—'

'Christos,' he corrected smoothly. 'Or if you prefer, just Chris. My friends call me Chris and so do my mother and sisters.'

'You have—relatives?' Somehow, that knowledge was most reassuring.

'Dozens,' he answered with some amusement. 'All Greeks have.'

'Because you all have so many children—' The words were out before she realised it, and although she stopped abruptly her companion uttered a low laugh and said, 'Our women are very fertile, yes.'

Julie coloured and wondered if he meant her to. She was beginning to think he was a strange, unpredictable man with many facets to his personality.

'You still haven't explained, Mr Dardanis,' she said after a pause. He turned right round to face her; she was vitally aware of the glint in the eyes that were subjecting her to an intense scrutiny.

'Julie,' he murmured softly, 'you'll oblige

48

me by doing as I say. Let me hear you call me Christos.'

She bit her lip, shook her head and said faintly, 'I can't, Mr Dardanis—it's impossible. I scarcely know you!'

'Say it,' he persisted, and as she found her eyes fixed to his, rather in the way a victim is held by a merciless predator, Julie was dazedly aware of saying, 'Christos . . .'

'Good girl! And don't forget, it is Christos—or Chris, all the time.'

'I don't understand!' she protested, then stopped and glanced around, half afraid she had attracted the attention of other passengers. Reassured, she spoke again, this time in a much lower and controlled tone of voice. 'Please explain, Mr—er—Christos.' She was hot all over, and scared of the mess she had landed herself in. Yet it was undoubtedly a wise decision at the time, since it meant escape from Mark. But of course, she had not visualised a situation such as this. To all intents and purposes she was to be on loan to this customer, to model clothes for him, until her services were no longer required, and then she would take up her job of secretary again in Bournemouth. All so simple and uncomplicated . . .

But not now. Julie felt she had landed

herself in the centre of some intrigue, and she was naturally wondering just what was to be expected of her.

More than modelling, that was for sure!

'I was intending to explain when we had arrived at my flat,' he was saying. And, after a small thoughtful pause, 'I feel that this will be best, Julie. Wait until we're settled in, and you've been reassured by my housekeeper, Maria, who is fifty-two and a widow. She's homely and she speaks very good English. No,' he said severely when she would have interrupted, 'I shan't brook any more questions, Julie. Wait, and if you then want to leave and return to England, there will be nothing to stop you.'

Nothing to stop her . . . That was reassuring enough, surely? And of course, Maria who was middle-aged and homely . . .

The apartment was a luxuriously appointed establishment in a small select block overlooking Constitution Square in Athens. Julie could not help but be enchanted with it, and especially with the bedroom she had been shown into by a smiling, buxom Greek woman who had insisted on unpacking for her and hanging her dresses in the wardrobe.

'The view is good? *Poli kala?*'

'Yes, very good.'

'Ah,' delightedly, 'you know meaning of *poli kala!* Very good!'

So she now knew how to say, 'very good'. Absurd to feel a lift of spirits simply because she'd learned a couple of Greek words. Not that her spirits were low in any case; she was already feeling happier, more secure. But of course there was that explanation to come, and she rather thought it might disturb her in no small measure.

Christos had said after introducing her to Maria, 'You'll want to settle in and perhaps tidy yourself, but then I'd like to see you in the salon—say in about an hour's time.'

Julie, impatient to have her curiosity satisfied, entered the salon a quarter of an hour early and so had time to look around, to appreciate the exquisite taste of the owner in such things as the tapestries on the walls, the gold and white ceiling from where two gleaming Waterford crystal chandeliers hung, one at each end of the large room. Plants grew from pewter urns or oak tubs bound with copper bands. The big easy chairs were covered with heavy cretonne to match the curtains, while the floor tiling was in a shade of rustic brown in contrast to

51

the blues and greens and yellows of the cretonne. Comfort was the object, and yet luxury was obvious. Julie walked over to examine some beautiful silver-gilt candlesticks and a snuffer that matched them. In a Regency cabinet were groups in finest porcelain—Chelsea and Meissen, delicate Bow and colourful Derby.

Julie swung around as Christos came in; he was dressed in casual slacks of oystergrey and a very light grey cotton shirt with the sleeves rolled up to the elbows. Bronzed and in the prime of his manhood, he made such an impressive and distinguished figure that Julie involuntarily caught her breath, deeply affected by the sheer perfection of the man. *He* ought to be a model, she thought, deciding that he was even more unbelievably handsome than any of the models for men's clothes she had seen in the glossy magazines.

He walked into the room, grace and confidence in every step he took.

'You are satisfied with your room?' No anxiety or doubt; he knew she could not be other than satisfied with such luxury and comfort.

'It's lovely,' she said, giving him a faint smile. 'The view is spectacular.'

He nodded, but absently, and flicked a hand, indicating a chair.

'Sit down,' he invited. 'We'll talk and then you shall make your decision. We'll dine out, I think,' he added with a glance at the Buhl clock sitting on the sideboard. 'It's late to be asking Maria to begin cooking.'

So considerate! A few days ago Julie had been hating this man with a black venom, but now she was willing to admit that there was an altogether different side to his personality from that which he had adopted at the 'fashion show'.

Having occupied the chair indicated, she folded her hands in her lap and waited, albeit not very patiently, for Christos to begin. He was standing, and this made her feel small and inferior, overwhelmed because the very atmosphere seemed to vibrate with his presence.

He came to within a couple of feet of where she sat, looked down at her for a long, silent moment and then, without a hint of warning, he said, 'I want you to be my pillow-friend, Julie.'

She gaped, half rising from the chair, her eyes widened to their fullest extent.

'Wh-what d-did you say?' she stammered, sinking down into the cushions again.

'I believe you understood, Julie.'

She shook her head from side to side, dazed and wondering if this were a dream. And yet . . . Hadn't she known he was interested in her body? But for all that, she could not fully accept that he had brought her here just to tell her this—tell her he wanted her for his mistress.

'I don't understand,' she managed, failing utterly to appear cool and collected, which she would dearly have liked to do. 'You can't be—be serious!'

He was smiling faintly, his deep-set tawny eyes alight with humour.

'Not quite categorically,' he assured her. 'I want you to act the part—'

'Act? Pretend to be your—your—er . . . ?'

'Exactly. I have a very good reason, I can assure you.'

'You must have!' tartly and with a little more courage. 'I'm sorry to disappoint you, Mr Dardanis, but you'll have to find someone else.'

The brown eyes were narrowed and glinting, and in spite of herself Julie felt a quickening of her nerves.

'Christos,' he said in a dangerously soft voice. 'Don't forget again.'

'It isn't necessary—not now. You assumed

I'd agree to your request, but I can't do it— and you can't make me,' she added for good measure.

'Can't I?' The tawny eyes flickered strangely, and although his manner was polished and suave, there was something almost threatening in the way he was looking at her, and there was a veiled quality in his tone when at length he spoke again. 'I usually get what I want, Julie . . . and I happen to want you to do this thing for me. You should consider my proposal carefully before making any snap decision; think carefully about every aspect; visualise how you will fare if you return to England—'

'How I'll fare?' she interrupted, watching him closely. It almost seemed that he knew something.

'Things might not always be what you would wish them to be. You could find yourself in difficulty.'

Her eyes grew veiled. It seemed that he did know something. And yet . . . how could he? How could he know that she would have difficulties if she went back home? She realised now that his condition that she must come along with the order was in effect a sort of blackmail to ensure he would get her over here. She now very much doubted if he would in fact have cancelled the order. Threatening to do so appeared to be nothing more nor less than a ruse.

She murmured at last, 'This good reason you mentioned, Mr—Christos?'

There was a momentary hesitation before he said, 'I'll try to be brief.'

But again he paused and, looking at him, at the flexed jaw and compressed lips, Julie fully appreciated his difficulty in proffering her an explanation. Yet at the same time he knew it was necessary if he were to succeed in persuading her to fall in with his plan, a plan that was as yet vague and baffling to Julie. She felt he could have easily have found someone else to pose as his mistress; the fact that he had not done so added to the mystery.

'It all began,' he continued presently, 'when my father and the father of a girl called Androula Perides arranged a marriage between Androula and me. We were both twelve years old—'

'Twelve!' exclaimed Julie, aghast. 'An *arranged* marriage? Surely they don't arrange marriages these days?'

'It was fifteen years ago. My father died in very great pain six years later, but before he died he made me promise solemnly that I would one day marry Androula. I was eighteen at the time and never even thought of going against Father's wishes—children didn't in those days, not in my country—'

'But arranged marriages!' Julie could not help interrupting again. 'Surely that kind of thing died out a long time ago?' She was intrigued and interested, and forgot for the moment that any of this concerned her.

'Today children don't allow themselves to be dictated to by parents—at least, not in the big towns, that is,' he agreed. 'But unfortunately, in the remote villages of Greece the dowry system and arranged marriages still survive, and strongly. Custom, you see, is difficult to break.' He moved away from her and sat down, his back to the window, his face for the moment a bronzed mask of detachment. He was obviously lost in thought and Julie waited patiently for him to continue.

'Fortunately for me, Father omitted to stipulate any date for the marriage when he extracted the promise from me. However, Androula's father wanted us married the following year.'

'When you were only nineteen?' Julie herself had been married at that age; it was far too young for a woman and absurdly young for a man.

He was nodding his head.

'I stalled because I was still studying at Athens University. But Mother was gradually becoming impatient; she reminded me over and over again of my promise. Androula too was quite naturally wanting to be married. Time went on; I began to realise that I would never love Androula, so I was honest and told her so, asking her to break the engagement, but she flatly refused.' Christos stopped and his mouth went tight, his eyes dark. 'I decided to go abroad and went to London, where I stayed for three years, managing a vast concern manufacturing women's gowns and other clothes.' He mentioned the name of the firm, known throughout the United Kingdom, and Julie nodded slowly. 'I then decided to utilise the money left me by my father to set up on my own. I returned to Greece and my new business as wholesaler prospered quite beyond my dreams. By this time it was fourteen years since the marriage had been arranged, and of course twenty-six was old for a Greek girl not to be married, but Androula had remained obstinate throughout the years.'

He gave a small sigh and again became

lost in thought, his eyes, though, straying in Julie's direction, and she noticed with a tiny frown of puzzlement the most odd expression in their depths, an unfathomable expression which she wished she could read.

'My mother has always been on her side and we are now becoming estranged—although to tell the truth we've never been really close. Androula's father persistently phones me, and writes, but I'm determined not to marry Androula.'

'Because you don't love her?' A strange story, Julie mused, commiserating with him, even though he did not appear to be a man needing pity—just the contrary, in fact.

'That's the most important reason. I'm sorry for her, in a way, yet she's single only through her own obstinacy. She's beautiful and could have had many chances of marriage.'

'Is she in love with you?' asked Julie, and a thin smile touched his lips.

'How can she be, when we've never seen much of each other at all? And we've never once been alone. No—' he shook his head firmly, 'Androula can't possibly be in love with me.'

Julie had to agree, and could not for the life of her understand why the girl should want to hold to his promise a man who had made it clear that he did not want to marry her. It didn't make sense, unless . . .

'Perhaps Androula still feels herself bound; she might be totally influenced by her father.'

'I agree. She is certainly influenced by her father, who in turn continually reminds me of my promise to my father, and considers I should waste no more time in honouring it.' Christos looked directly at Julie and continued, his accented voice low but firm, 'I want you to pose as my pillow-friend because the fact that I have openly taken a woman under my protection, as we call it here, will instantly shock all concerned. It is my opinion that neither Androula nor her father will persist in upholding our engagement. And once it's broken I'm let out, for good.'

Julie, with a little shock of surprise, discovered that she really wanted to help Christos. Yet a frown knitted her brow at the idea of people believing she was living with Christos as his mistress. She squirmed at the thought, even though the people concerned were strangers to her.

'Your mother,' she queried, playing for time, 'she too will be—be shocked?'

60

'Very.'

'But,' said Julie as the thought occurred to her, 'don't all Greek men have—er—pillow-friends? And isn't it usually overlooked?'

'An engaged man is not supposed to take a pillow-friend. He's supposed to remain faithful to his betrothed.'

Julie sent him an oblique glance and asked, 'Have you been faithful all the time, Christos?'

To her surprise the ghost of an amused smile touched the hard outline of his mouth. She had half expected some haughty rebuke or snub for putting a question of that nature.

'I'm almost twenty-eight, Julie.' He shook his head and the smile deepened. 'No, I haven't been faithful.'

Julie flushed, and he laughed. She caught her breath suddenly. What a transformation when he laughed like that! He was very human all at once, and devastatingly attractive.

'What puzzles me,' she frowned after a while, 'is why you chose me for this—pose?'

Silence, intense and profound. She felt her nerves tighten as the uncanny hush continued. Christos had been staring at her, but

61

now he was looking through the window to the brittle blue sky where fair-weather clouds floated about like lace fashioned from cobwebs. A typical Grecian sky, Julie was soon to learn.

He spoke at last, after she had stirred restlessly in her chair.

'I thought that I would say we'd been lovers for several years, when I was living in London. Had I chosen a Greek girl I couldn't have said that, simply because I wasn't living in Greece.' He looked at her again. 'I estimated your age at around twenty-four, so it meant I'd be quite safe in saying we'd been lovers for several years.'

'I'm twenty-five,' she said, and then, 'Is there some advantage in your saying the affair has been going on for years?' She stopped somewhat abruptly, stunned by the fact that she was subconsciously seeing herself in the role he wanted her to play.

'Yes, of course. A long-standing affair will appear far more permanent than something that could be regarded as trivial. They'll all assume that, even if I did agree to marry Androula, I'd be unlikely to give up a girl who'd managed to retain my interest for several years.'

Julie had to smile, and Christos responded.

'You appear to have it worked out to perfection,' she said rather dryly.

'I feel sure it will work,' he assured her.

'Perhaps you're right.'

'Julie . . . are you going to help me?' Serious the tone and in his eyes expectancy. 'I feel it will be beneficial to you to remain in Greece for the time being.'

She just had to say, 'Christos, do you know anything about my background?'

'Nothing concrete, Julie, but the fact of your leaving the gap of about six years when you were telling me about yourself convinced me that you have a secret. It is not my affair, but I rather think that something that has happened recently caused you to change your mind—and it was nothing to do with the fact that perhaps some of your colleagues might be put out of work—' He broke off and shrugged his broad shoulders. 'I might be wrong, of course, but it did strike me that you had been told that one of the factories would have to be put on short time if I didn't place that order.'

Julie merely nodded and wondered just how much Christos had guessed about her. She felt sure he had no idea she was married, but certain that he suspected she had been in some trouble and so had agreed to come to Greece in order to get away from it. He guessed, too, that were she to return to England the trouble would immediately face her again, hence the confidence he appeared to have in being able to make her stay. He was waiting for an answer to the question he had put to her a few moments ago, and she heard herself say, quietly and without a tremor in her voice, 'I'll help you, Christos.' But she had to add, a blush rising to her cheeks, 'It'll be very embarrassing, though, if I have to meet your mother. And I don't know how you're to convince her you have a—a—pillow-friend unless you produce her.'

He gave a tiny sigh and his frown was deep. The look in his eyes was unfathomable.

'I know it will be difficult for you, Julie, because you will have to meet more than my mother. You do fully understand?'

'You mean I shall have to meet Androula and her father?' A shudder passed through her at this idea.

'I'm afraid so—and my sisters and some of my friends.'

Julie bit her lip till it hurt. She wanted to withdraw . . . and yet, paradoxically, she wanted to help Christos gain his freedom from an engagement that never should have been arranged at all.

'I expect I'll survive.' She tried to make her voice sound light and failed miserably, and to her astonishment Christos rose, came towards her, and before she knew it her wrist had been taken in a warm hand and she was pulled gently to her feet. With his other hand Christos tilted her chin and the next moment his lips were warm and moist on hers. She stared into his eyes when he released her, and tried to look shocked. He said softly, 'Thank you, Julie. Yes, you'll survive, for you have me with you, remember. I shall make sure you are never alone in any of these people's company.'

So they could never have a chance of insulting her, he was saying.

'Shall I be required to model the dresses—?' She stopped, for it seemed ludicrous to bring up a subject like that at a time like this.

He slanted her a glance of amusement and asked,

'Do you want to?'

'I don't really know,' she answered candidly.

'Then let us leave it for the time being.

And now, let me take you out to dine. The Plaka's the place, as I know of a delightful *taverna* there where there's *bouzouki* music and Greek dancing while we eat.'

'I'd like that,' she said eagerly, and a surge of happiness washed over her in a way she would never have believed possible only a few short days ago. 'Shall I be all right in this dress?' It was a shirtwaister in twilled cotton, light green in colour, and she wore a thin gold chain, short, so that it fell just into the open neckline. Her hair had been vigorously brushed till it shone and she had touched her pale cheeks with blusher, a flattering jewel colour meant just for evenings.

'You look splendid,' Christos assured her. 'Just right for the informal atmosphere of the Plaka.'

Chapter Four

It was only to be expected that Julie would be tense and on edge when, just a week after they had come from England, Christos—whom she now called Chris after some further persuasion from him—told her his mother was coming to Athens and would be staying overnight at the flat.

'I'm terrified!' she admitted, uncaring that he would consider her attitude melodramatic. 'How on earth are you going to explain?'

'Just leave everything to me,' he replied with his customary calm. 'Take your cues, but don't talk much. Remember my promise: I shall never leave you alone with any of the people concerned.' Chris was very busy, had been all week—but today he had come home from the office early and suggested they dine out in the Plaka again. Julie agreed, but she did wonder if this treat was a sort of conscience present because she had had such short notice of his mother's visit.

They went out into the teeming night life of Athens, walking through a labyrinth of narrow alleys, where a hotch-potch of *tavernas* and shops and clubs looked very much to Julie as if they had once been houses, perhaps in medieval times. Lanterns and strings of fairy lights gave the whole place an atmosphere of festival time. Cafés were filled to overflowing with both tourists and Greeks; all kinds of odours filled the air, mainly from kebabs cooking on charcoal stoves; but there were perfumes too, from the flower sellers who offered jasmine and gardenias, trying to pin them on to people's clothing so that they would be forced to buy. Chris pushed them off with a heavy hand, and for a short while his other hand held Julie's, so that he could keep her with him in the mass of people thronging the streets.

At last they came to the *taverna* where they had eaten before, and as Chris had phoned for a booking they were instantly conducted to a table close to the raised dais on which the dancers would perform.

'A good place for you, Mr Christos,' smiled the stocky waiter, showing the inevitable gold fillings. His dark eyes were roving Julie's figure and she was reminded of Angela's saying that Greek men mentally strip a woman of her clothing. She turned from his lecherous stare to take the chair Chris had pulled out for her. As she sat down his face seemed to come close to her hair, and absurdly she was glad she was wearing her new, exotic perfume which a colleague had recently brought her back from the Caribbean, and which was described on the label as 'capturing the essence of the islands'.

A hint of colour tinted her cheeks, infused there by her thoughts, and Chris, noticing it, lifted an eyebrow enquiringly and said, 'Something wrong?' which didn't help at all, and to her vexation Julie felt her colour heighten even more.

'No, nothing,' she answered, and to her relief he picked up the menu and began to peruse it. As on the previous occasion he described the Greek food to her. They both ordered moussaka and fresh green salads with several other side dishes. The wine was a French dry white and the dessert a compôte of spiced fruit. During the meal four men danced several times, accepting flowers from the women sellers and putting them behind their ears. Chris had already explained that Greek dancing related to the pagan Dionysian rites depicted on the ancient vases found in graves all over Greece.

'Is it always men who dance?' asked Julie, and her companion nodded and explained that the women were far too tired to take part in such vigorous movements. But he did amend this by adding, 'There are dances in which women take part, but it is more often the men who dance.'

The four men were linked together by a handkerchief, twisted and knotted. The leader leapt high into the air, then landing lightly on his feet he rocked and dipped in almost frenzied movements, his eyes lifted to the ceiling of vines, a sort of ecstasy in their depths. The handkerchief was used to link them again after this solo performance and the four danced together. Then the leader again—this time dropping to the floor and elevating his groin, rotating it in sensuous movements which brought the flush of embarrassment once again to Julie's face. Chris flicked her a glance and she noticed the amused curve of his lips. What a sexy lot these Greek men were!

The leader was still performing on his own, in even more abandonment, his body now dripping sweat as his levitations seemed to afford him a sort of quivering ecstasy. He tore the handkerchief to shreds, staring unseeingly at it as if he were lost in a world of sublime joy. The *bouzouki* music continued for a few seconds after he had stopped, having sunk to the floor, balancing low on his right foot, with his left leg extended. It was a sensuous pose, and Julie was relieved when the four men at last took their bow, to tremendous applause. The Greeks were a noisy race, she thought, and yet Chris was very different—quiet and aristocratic, a patrician among all these plebeians.

He was looking quizzically at her as he supplied her with more wine.

'You didn't enjoy the dancing?'

'In a way I did.' She felt shy and vexed because of it. This man overwhelmed her with his superiority, his air of distinction. She found herself wondering what kind of a woman he would eventually marry—whether she would be like him, haughty and rather cold and unemotional, with that dispassionate air about her which was so much a part of Chris's make-up.

During the past week she had paraded some samples which he had brought back with him from Copelands, also some others he had had sent from two London firms. He had sat there, watching her critically, then glancing around at the potential customers to see what effect the show was having on them. At work he was a totally different man—the man she had first met at Copelands when his attitude had aroused her anger so much that she had told herself—and several colleagues—that she hated him.

Well, she did not hate him now; something had happened to her and she found herself repeatedly refusing to analyse the effect this noble Greek was having on her.

They arrived back at the flat well after midnight; the wine had been heady and Julie was in the grip of a contented languor, feeling that life was not so bad after all. Chris looked at her, examining her face through narrowed eyes . . . and suddenly she was fully awake and alert. He came slowly across the room; she said swiftly as she backed away, 'It's very late—I'll s-say goodnight—'

'Not yet, my dear.' He was close beside her now and she felt her heart lurch. 'It's early—not yet one o'clock.'

'I'm tired.' She took another strategic step backwards and noticed the ironic smile that curved his lips.

'And . . . afraid?' he drawled, watching her fluctuating colour through narrowed eyes.

'Afraid?' with well-simulated enquiry. 'What is there to be afraid of?'

Chris gave a gust of laughter, so a few seconds elapsed before he spoke.

'You do very well, my dear, but you are afraid. It's plain—'

'I'm going to bed!' She made for the door, but Chris leapt towards her with the agility of a tiger and grasped her wrist, his hold tightening as she began to struggle. 'You shouldn't be so tempting,' he said suavely as he forced her to come close to his tall, lithe body. He looked down into her flushed face; she wondered if he was aware of how quickly her heart was beating. Something in the way he was looking at her caused her to frown and for a fleeting moment forget the immediate danger she was in. For he seemed to be examining her speculatively, endeavouring to make some sort of guess—or assessment, and for no explicable reason she was reminded of his mentioning the six years' gap she had left when telling him about herself.

'Let me go . . . please.' Her face was pale, disturbed as with a rush of painful thoughts, of bitter recollections, she almost relived that last hateful night with her husband. 'I w-want to go to bed.'

'You said you weren't afraid,' he reminded her, and his voice was gentle, his expression a trifle anxious. 'Don't be, Julie, my dear. I shan't hurt you.' His hold on her wrist slackened, but his arm went about her waist and as he continued to stare into her eyes she knew he was going to kiss her.

It was a gentle touch of the lips, and his hand caressed her silken hair.

'If you'll let me go,' she began . . . even while, quite suddenly, she wanted to stay, just like this, close but without passion, and she realised that this comfort was what she had so desperately wanted from Mark, a physical comfort afforded by the strength and warmth of his body, yet without any sexual desires on either side. Surely this had not been asking too much of her husband after her terrible loss? True, Mark had also been devastated, but somehow he had soon seemed to recover and because of this he was totally unable to understand her own crucifying agony, much less sympathise with it. Unknowingly she shivered, and Chris's arm tightened around her.

'You're distressed about something,' he murmured, his breath cool and fresh on her cheek. 'Would you like to tell me all about it?'

'About it?' Her eyes were no longer troubled and her heart-rate had settled down to normal.

'Those six years—or rather, what happened during that time?' But she was shaking her head even before he finished speaking.

'You wouldn't be interested,' she said, and pulled away from his hold.

'It's because I'm interested that I asked you to confide.'

Again she shook her head.

'I don't want to talk, Chris—' She twisted around. 'I'm going to bed now.'

'All right.' His smile was crooked, faintly amused. 'I won't tempt you, my dear.'

Julie had turned towards the door, but she swung around at his words, spoken with an undercurrent of total confidence.

'You believe you could?' she challenged, then instantly became uneasy.

Chris's voice was gently taunting as he replied, that crooked smile still in evidence, 'Be careful, Julie; I might just take up the gauntlet.'

'I didn't mean to—I wasn't—er . . .'

'. . . daring me?' One eyebrow quirked as he laughed. 'It sounded very much like it.' He paused a moment. 'You're too sensitive,' he asserted unexpectedly. 'You must have had a most unhappy experience.'

She was silent, standing close to the door, but with her body turned towards him. She felt sure he had no idea she was married, which meant that he was assuming she had had an unhappy experience with some man other than a husband. This made her feel ashamed, embarrassed, and for a moment she toyed with the idea of telling him the truth. Yet something urged her to silence regarding that part of her life, and it was not until later that she was to realise that she did not want Chris to know she was a married woman.

She had opened the door when he said, very quietly, 'Come here, Julie.'

Her heart began to race again.

'No—I'm—'

'I said come here.'

To her own surprise she obeyed, walking over to where he stood, his back to the window. Her stare was enquiring and he seemed amused. But Julie noticed other things besides the half-smile curving his lips and the dancing light in his eyes. She saw the strength of the firm chin and the hard, inflexible line of his jaw, the straight dark brows below a faintly lined forehead. The black hair cut into it in a well marked widow's peak. A man to command respect— but then she had deduced this at their very first meeting. A man no one would cross swords with unless they could not possibly help it.

He pointed a finger to bring her closer and again she obeyed.

'You're no longer afraid,' he stated, and took her face between his hands. 'I'm glad,' he added and, bending his head, he kissed her lips, prolonging the pleasure it afforded him until, breathless, she pushed with urgency against his chest. He looked down into her face, aware of quivering lips and eyes that were moist, and an unfathomable expression crossed his features, as if some emotion had suddenly caught him in its grip, an emotion which he had every intention of hiding behind the mask. Julie quivered within the circle of his arms, feeling secure even while aware of the first stirrings of desire, a yearning which she knew instinctively she ought to be vanquishing while she still had the power, because undoubtedly this man was dangerous, gentle though he might be, and, somehow, anxious about her. Yet she made no protest when, with a casualness that rendered the action almost automatic, he trailed a line from her cheek to her throat, then to her breast where his hand spread, then closed. Quivers of ecstasy brought added warmth to her body, increasing as his hand roved the tender curves from waist to thigh, while the other hand tightened to harden her breast. His mouth was moist and possessive, crushing her lips with a passion she had never known before—no, not in all those years with Mark. What had she missed? Why was this so different? Why was the blood racing through her veins, her pulses throbbing so that every cell in her body seemed to be affected?

'You're . . . beautiful.' His voice had a throaty sound and his breath was hot now against her mouth. 'Let's go to your room.' So casual, except for the ardour edging his voice. Julie managed to draw away even while she felt trapped by the sheer masculine power of him, the magnetism which for a moment had made her forget all but the primitive desire to let him go further . . . and further . . .

'No! I don't know how you can make such a suggestion! What about Maria?'

The last three words seemed to amuse him, but his manner was serious as he replied, bringing her to him again,

'Maria has gone to bed, hours ago.' He held her gaze, while his sensuously probing fingers slid almost arrogantly through her hair, his whole manner masterful, possessive, as if he were some mighty Greek deity and she a mere mortal, subservient to his will . . . and his demands, whatever they might prove to be. Julie quivered within the arms that held her, held her strongly against his frame so that she was vitally aware of his need, the throbbing sensuality of his maleness and, helpless against the primitive draw and the desire, she arched her body, shaping it to his, rapture coming closer and closer as his roving hands found tender places, stroking and pressing until she was crazy with desire for fulfilment. His mouth, rough and masterful, found the sweetness of silken cheeks before closing over her own mouth, with a primordial passion that made her think she was caught in a tornado sending her to dizzy heights which could only lead to paradise.

'I want you . . .' Her words were silently spoken, and yet, paradoxically, she wished he could have heard them. What was the matter with her, that she could be so abandoned as this . . . and not even put up some form of resistance, however feeble and half-hearted?

'Are we going to your bedroom?' Chris's voice was throaty again, betraying a certain weakness, she thought, the weakness assailing a man on the very edge of rapture. But the question again affected her adversely and she managed to draw from his arms.

She shook her head, but before she had time to speak he was cupping her face with hands that were both tender and possessive.

'We need each other, Julie,' he said with a confidence that brought a sudden frown to her brow. 'It's too late to draw back now, you must agree?'

Again she shook her head, wishing her nerves and her heart would settle. Her breathing was erratic, too, and desire was still strong within her. How easy it would be to surrender! But what of tomorrow, when Chris would look at her with contempt? An easy victim, another scalp for his belt. An interlude to be enjoyed and then forgotten. Somehow she was given the strength to say,

'I don't agree, Chris. I don't know what came over me—'

'Not that!' he broke in, amused. 'Pretence is futile at this stage. We shan't be doing anything wrong if we enjoy a few hours together.'

'You're so casual about it!' Julie moved away, surprised that she was allowed to put so much distance between them. His gaze was steadfastly focused on her, searching her eyes as if he would read what was in her mind; then his glance was roving over her, and she blushed in the knowledge that he was aware of her laboured breathing, because the rise and fall of her breasts was plain for him to see.

'Casual?' He seemed not quite to understand that. 'What do you want me to do—act as if I love you?'

She flinched. It was as if an icy shower were directed at her, and yet her cheeks were burning.

'No,' she managed to say, but in a quivering voice. 'Naturally I don't expect that, any more than you expect anything so absurd from me.' She turned to the door. 'Goodnight,' she added, and, to her amazement, she was allowed to open it and leave the room.

Had he been angry? It seemed not to be the case. Perhaps he had suddenly decided to let caution ascend over all else because he was depending so very greatly on her co-operation. Should she change her mind then he would have gone to an enormous amount of trouble for nothing. Yes, that was the explanation for his letting her go without further argument or persuasion.

Julie undressed, had a quick shower and got into bed, and all the time she found herself unable to accept that explanation; within her subconscious there was the conviction that Chris had some altogether different motive for letting her go unharmed.

'Mr Christos—your mother.' Maria had

opened the door but, almost before she had announced Mrs Dardanis, the woman had swept into the room.

'Don't be absurd, Maria! I do not need to be announced.' She flicked the housekeeper an arrogant glance before adding something in Greek which caused Maria to colour hotly. Julie, tensed already, shot a glance at Chris and saw his eyes darken with anger at the way his housekeeper was being treated.

'*Matera* . . .' He rose from his chair by the window, tall and impressive as any statue of a Greek god. His mouth was set, his jaw taut. 'I hope you are well?'

'I'm always well—' her eyes were on Julie, sitting there, her heart pounding wildly against her ribs; this woman was far more formidable than her son at his most severe. Tall and stately, wearing clothes that had clearly come from Paris, with gold chains at her throat and wrist, and diamonds and sapphires gleaming on her long, perfectly-manicured hands, she tossed a Gucci handbag on to the sofa with a careless gesture, but her dark, piercing eyes remained on Julie. Chris, who had seemed incredibly undisturbed, flicked a hand and said smoothly,

'Mother, meet Julie . . . my friend. Julie, my *matera*.'

'How do you do,' said Julie, rising and coming forward with outstretched hand. 'I'm very happy to meet you.' She hoped that was the correct thing to say and wished belatedly that she had sought advice from Chris about this first meeting with his mother.

'Your . . . friend?' sharply, as Mrs Dardanis's eyes widened in something like disbelief. She glanced down at the hand which Julie had offered, and made no attempt to take it. 'What exactly do you mean?' She added something in Greek, but, watching Chris closely, Julie could gain nothing of its meaning; if it had further angered him then he had no intention of revealing the fact. Julie withdrew her hand and sat down.

'Do sit down, Mother—'

'When I'm ready. What friend is this— and why haven't I heard of her before?'

'Julie and I have been friends . . . very good friends, for several years. I thought it was time I brought her here, to live with me.' So calm and suave! Julie gasped at the sheer self-confidence of the man. He was still standing and he flicked a hand indicating a chair. 'Sit down,' he said, and now there was an edge of impatience in his voice.

His mother stood and glowered at Julie, whose cheeks were hot, her eyes downcast. Never would she have believed she could feel quite so ashamed and embarrassed as this. True, she had known that to some extent she would experience some sense of shame when confronted with Chris's mother, but this . . . Chris should have warned her what his mother was like and what to expect of her. The dark piercing eyes were filled with contempt, but there was consternation there, too, and certainly anger. She turned her attention to her son and when she spoke her voice had a high-pitched tone that brought a frown to Chris's already darkened brow.

'I don't think I understand, Christos. You're betrothed—or have you forgotten?'

He shook his head.

'Certainly I haven't forgotten,' was his taut reply. 'There are too many people who are determined I shan't forget.'

'Then this woman—' She flipped a hand, her voice reflecting her anger and contempt. 'You can't have her living here!'

'She is living here—No, Julie, don't go,' he added imperiously as she rose from her

84

chair, feeling unable to tolerate any more. *This woman,* indeed! She met Chris's hard stare and managed to say calmly, 'I feel you and your mother can discuss the situation far better without my presence.'

'Darling,' he murmured softly, his tender gaze, assumed for his mother's benefit, affecting Julie in a way that set her heart racing. 'Do sit down. Mother would have to know some time that you and I are lovers, and have been for some years.' He looked at his mother, who was still standing, her dark face twisted and her eyes flashing with condemnation.

'How long is "some years"?' she demanded harshly.

'Does it matter?' with an arrogant lift of his straight black brows. 'And now, Mother, we'll change the subject, if you don't mind. I'm not having Julie treated with anything but respect—'

'Respect!' snapped his mother, sitting down at last. 'It's the first time I've been asked to respect one of your pillow-friends!'

Julie flinched but shot Chris a glance. Surely that sort of statement would throw him into some degree of confusion. But no. He was as cool as ever as he replied,

'Julie is different. Remember we've been

together for several years. The tie is stronger than with any of the others . . . and always will be,' he added slowly and emphatically. 'I shall never give her up.'

'But when you are married to Androula—' His mother's white teeth snapped together as a hissing sound escaped her. 'You *will* give this woman up!' she snapped. 'And at once! It's time you were married—I saw Androula's father last week and we both decided the delay has gone on long enough. The marriage will be arranged for the middle of next month.' She spoke with a finality that troubled Julie who, despite her almost unbearable discomfiture, was glad she had agreed to help Chris. An arranged marriage for a man of his age was unbelievable.

But she had no need to worry. Chris, having risen from his chair, literally stood over his mother, an impenetrable, uncompromising air about him and a certain arrogance which, to Julie, seemed to add to the attraction he now had for her, and it was with a shock of surprise that she was admitting that she was becoming far more drawn to him than was wise. The present conversation had strengthened her conviction that he had had many women; hadn't he told his mother that Julie was tied to him more strongly than 'any of the others?' How many others? But what was it to her? When she had served her purpose Chris would thank her, bid her a cheerful goodbye and pay her air fare back to England.

He was speaking, in tones dangerously quiet but which made Julie shiver all the same. She was glad it wasn't her with whom he was angry.

'I said, Mother, that we will change the subject. What I do is my own affair; I am captain of my own actions, and if you've been both foolish and presumptuous enough to have discussed an early marriage between Androula and me, then you have wasted your time—you and Androula's father. I've given her every chance of freedom; she could have been married long ago if she'd had any sense.' He glinted down into the face as arrogant as his own. 'If I ever marry Androula, it will be in my own good time, and as I said, I shall not give up Julie.'

His mother's anger threatened to render her speechless, as it was a long time before she spoke.

'You seem to have forgotten your promise to your dying father. Or don't you care that you flout his wishes?' She paused, but her son's face was inscrutable. 'You do realise,' she went on harshly, 'that you can never break your engagement to Androula?'

He nodded instantly.

'I'm fully aware of the rules,' he replied smoothly. 'I shall not break them.' His manner was almost nonchalant, designed, Julie suspected, to annoy his mother even further. Her eyes were ablaze with anger, her mouth tightly compressed. She threw a glance of utter dislike in Julie's direction before saying slowly, 'This woman—'

'Julie!' he snapped.

'You say you've been friends for a number of years. You can't want to marry her. Greeks never marry their pillow-friends.'

Julie went hot, and this time when she rose she made straight for the door, and even when Chris authoritatively spoke her name she lifted her head in the air and marched from the room.

Hateful creature! How did a woman like that come to have a son like Chris? He certainly wasn't like her in any way, not even in looks. Arrogant he might be, and more sure of himself than most men, but his manners were impeccable, while his mother's were appalling.

Still hot, Julie went to her bedroom and stepped out on to the balcony. Down below in the Square was hurry and bustle; she wondered where all the people came from. There seemed to be millions of them, scurrying to get somewhere, or strolling aimlessly—men with their arms about each other, girls linking arms. And the traffic—it was chaotic! Thousands of car roofs shining in the sunlight, and policemen trying to control them. In the Square centre an outdoor café was crowded to capacity, its bright umbrellas turning slowly, caught by a zephyr of a breeze. Trees and flowers and stray dogs . . . A fascinating city, surely one of the most fascinating in the world, with its ancient ruins of temples and shrines, its sloping terrain, and the hill of Lycabettus rising to a brittle Grecian sky.

Restless, Julie turned away at last, wishing this disturbance within her could be clearly understood. Somehow, her life had become aimless; she had no job, no reason for activity. She wondered if 'pillow-friends' were always content to do nothing other than wait for their lovers to come to them. She was determined to talk to Chris and tell him she must be employed—although she certainly had no wish to be used as a model.

But she might persuade him to employ

her in his office where she could do the job to which she was accustomed.

She heard his step and swung around, her eyes fixed on the handle of the door. It turned after he had knocked just once.

'Julie,' he began in a troubled tone, 'I'm sorry.' He gave a small sigh. 'How does one apologise for the rudeness of others?'

'It's all right—I mean, I'm okay now. I was furious—and had every reason to be,' she told him crossly.

'I did tell you Mother would not be pleased.' He came further into the room, a charm about him that sent an emotion fluttering through her nerves.

'You did,' she agreed, 'but you didn't warn me about the sort of person she is.'

'To be honest, I didn't expect her to be quite so hostile towards you,' Chris confessed.

'She must think a lot of Androula.'

He nodded his dark head.

'She's extremely fond of her,' he agreed.

'What did she say about my being English?'

'Nothing; she wouldn't care what nationality my pillow-friends were so long as I marry a Greek woman.'

'Is she staying the night? I mean, she hasn't changed her mind?'

'No, she's staying. She has some friends to meet, and some shopping to do. She does this periodically.'

'Where does she live?' Julie asked.

'On the island of Paros. It's in the Cyclades.'

'Not very big?'

'No, not very big at all.'

'I should have thought she'd want to live on a larger island, like Rhodes or Crete.'

'Our family home has always been on Paros,' he told her. 'I have a home, though, on the island of Cos, which has a much larger population.'

Julie was interested.

'I remember reading that Cos has a rather wonderful history, and some marvellous antiquities.'

'That's right.' Chris paused a moment, as if undecided, and then, 'Would you like to go there some time, Julie?'

She hesitated. Chris was far too attractive; he drew her in a way that was not safe; she had no wish to become his pillow-friend in reality.

'I don't think so,' she began, when he stopped her by laughing.

'Afraid? There's no need to be, I assure you.'

'Candidly, I don't set much store by your assurances,' she was swift to retort, and again he laughed.

'After that romantic interlude? Well, it won't happen again . . . unless you want it to.' His eyes were gleaming with amusement, his lip curved in a slanting smile. 'You're different,' he stated unexpectedly, and came a step nearer to where she stood. 'An old-fashioned girl—or are you? I'd very much like to know about those six years, Julie.'

Was this the chance to put him off once and for all? If she were to tell him she was married would that be effective in keeping him at arms' length? It could very well be . . .

But did she really want to keep him at arms' length? A frown suddenly creased her brow as she became angry with herself and with the treacherous thoughts which had come to the forefront of her mind.

'I think we should change the subject,' she almost snapped. 'Can you find me some employment in your office? As you know, I was private secretary to Mr Holding, so I'm experienced in office work.'

'Don't you want to model? I'm having a show at the Grande Bretagne Hotel in about three weeks' time; I thought you might like to model the smaller size clothes?'

'Like?' with a lift of her brows. 'You know very well I didn't enjoy parading about in front of your . . .' She stopped, and a smile curved his lips.

' . . . critical eyes?' Chris finished for her, and she shot him a smouldering glance.

'It wasn't funny!'

'Indeed not.' His voice was suddenly grave. 'You were perfect. Anyone would assume you'd had training.'

Her glance had a quality of suspicion about it as she replied, 'I can't call you a liar, but all the same, I'm sure you're not honest.'

He shook his head, amused.

'That was a bit mixed, wasn't it? I'm not a liar but I don't tell the truth?'

Julie had to laugh; it eased the tenseness within her, and she was able to return lightly, 'You're so clever, Chris. You know very well what I was trying to say.'

'Perhaps,' he conceded, and then, more briskly, 'So you prefer the office to the glamour? All right, I'll see what I can do. I can't have you being bored, because this business might take some time.' He was frowning as he said this, and a sigh escaped him.

'How long?' she queried, her feelings mixed because on the one hand she knew that as her situation was dangerous she ought to want Chris's plan to mature quickly, on the other hand she knew she would be feeling more than a little depressed at the idea of saying a final goodbye to this dark Greek whose superlative looks and personality affected her more strongly than her husband's ever had. But of course, the circumstance that loomed more largely than anything else was the threats made by Mark, that he would find her wherever she was. So if she could stay away from England for perhaps a year or even more, his intention of persecuting her could very well have subsided.

'That is something I can't predict.' Chris's voice was taut. 'Both Androula and her father are obstinate and might prolong the issue, but on the other hand they could be so shocked that the betrothal could end immediately they know I have my—er—friend living with me.' He was laughing with his eyes, yet he seemed sympathetic when he saw her blush. 'Do you want it all to end soon, Julie?' he asked curiously, his dark eyes holding hers in what was a plain, unvarnished challenge that brought a constrained pause on Julie's part before she was able to reply, 'I don't frankly know, Chris.' Her eyes were wide and appealing. 'There are reasons why I ought to stay out of England for a while.'

He nodded slowly.

'I thought so. However,' he added, still in that curious and demanding tone, 'that is not what I meant, and you know it. If there was no reason for your being out of England at this time, would you want to leave here . . . leave me, and go back?' The implication was obvious, and Julie lowered her lashes, unaware of the added allure this action brought to her face.

'Just what are you asking me?' she prevaricated, and was not surprised to see a twisted smile appear on his lips.

'You and I have a certain attraction for one another,' he remarked, evading a direct answer to her question. 'So I firmly believe you'd not be eager to leave just yet awhile.'

Julie hesitated; she had always been incurably honest and knew she could never with truth deny that Chris did have a certain attraction for her. In fact, she was profoundly conscious of the attraction being far stronger than she would have wished; it was becoming so powerful that she was afraid to analyse its true meaning, since she was not convinced that the attraction—on her side—was altogether physical. On Chris's side, yes, it was purely a sexual urge, a primitive desire for her body.

A little cough reminded her that he was waiting for her comment, and although she shook her head, she had to confess,

'We do have an attraction for one another, Chris. But I have no intention of going any further than this sham. I'm your—er—friend in name only.' That sounded so utterly absurd that she had to laugh, and it was at the same time as he did. Their eyes danced as they met. Chris moved closer to take her face between his hands.

'I'm going to kiss you, nevertheless,' he stated, and suited the action to the words.

Chapter Five

To Julie's consternation Mrs Dardanis was sitting at the table when she came into the breakfast room. Julie had deliberately taken her time over bathing and dressing so that Chris would be there, avoiding finding herself alone with his mother. Where was Chris? Surely he would have on his mind the fact that a situation like this must never occur. He had promised never to leave her alone with anyone, yet here she was, with the woman who was surely the most hostile of any she would be likely to meet.

'*Kalimera.*' The greeting was coldly abrupt; Julie's response was equally cold.

'Good morning, Mrs Dardanis.' She hesitated, glancing backwards towards the door.

'Sit down.' The woman flicked an imperious hand on which the diamonds and emeralds gleamed. She was immaculate and severe in her dress and there was not a single hair out of place. 'Chris was called to the telephone.'

Julie sat down opposite her and shook out her napkin.

'You were here early,' she observed, her eyes on the woman's almost empty plate. She felt awkward and had spoken mainly to break the oppressive silence.

'I always rise early.' The hard eyes flicked over Julie's pale face contemptuously. 'But then I go to sleep early.'

Julie blushed but maintained an outward calm as she dug a spoon into the grapefruit which Maria had already put before her.

'Are you staying long?' she enquired after another lengthy silence had begun to affect her.

Mrs Dardanis flashed her an arrogant glance before replying, 'That is my business. Perhaps I can ask you the same question?'

'I shall be living here permanently,' answered Julie without meeting the woman's eyes.

'How long have you been my son's mistress?' The harshness in the tone accentuated the foreign accent, but the woman's English was excellent.

'Some years.' Julie was determined not to falter in her replies; she had no intention of giving Mrs Dardanis any cause for suspicion. She was keenly alert, Julie decided, and probably looking for any flaws in her son's story.

'How many years?'

Julie glanced up, her eyes sparkling.

'Does it matter?' she countered, and the older woman's mouth compressed.

'You're insolent! I intend to see that my son honours the promise he made to his father. He shall marry the girl he is betrothed to.'

'I believe he has always been willing to honour the promise.'

'Then why isn't he married to Androula? Why has he brought you here?'

'You'll have to ask Chris about that,' evaded Julie, leaning back as Maria came forward to pour her coffee.

Another silence ensued before Mrs Dardanis asked tautly, 'How much does my son pay you for your—er—services? I mean,' she added swiftly as Julie's eyes flamed with anger, 'what is your allowance?'

Julie said quiveringly, 'It's you who are insolent!' Her eyes raked the other woman with an expression of cold contempt. 'Another question to put to Chris, who no doubt will give you an answer of some kind.'

The hostility in the atmosphere could now be cut, and Julie turned her head again to see if Chris was coming. Why was he so long?

'I had a good reason for asking you the question.' Mrs Dardanis followed the direction of Julie's gaze and it was plain that, unlike Julie, she had no wish for her son's speedy return. 'I have thought of a proposition which I now put to you. I will pay you five years' allowance if you will pack up and leave here.'

Julie's eyes opened wide. This was something which Chris had not visualised, and some imp of mischief made Julie return, 'Mrs Dardanis, I'm sure you wouldn't be willing to pay me such an enormous sum of money.' The words were scarcely out when Julie regretted them. What on earth had come over her? Where was the acute embarrassment she had assumed she would feel if ever she found herself alone with Chris's mother?

'An enormous sum, eh?' repeated Mrs Dardanis sceptically. 'So you have your wits about you, it seems, but then all women of your particular trade are alert to the main chance. Well, miss, state your price and I'll consider it!'

All women of your particular trade . . . Black fury rose chokingly right up into Julie's throat, preventing speech. Never could she remember feeling she would like to strike someone, but that was how she felt at this moment. Mrs Dardanis had begun to repeat her last sentence when Chris strode in, an apology for Julie on his lips. He saw the two bright spots of colour on her cheeks, the sparkle in her eyes; he lowered his to stare at the little fist clenched on the table, clenched so tightly that the knucklebones seemed almost to be ready to break through the skin. His narrowed eyes sought his mother's, but she was looking down, at the last bit of bacon on her plate. He sat down; Maria put his breakfast before him—eggs and bacon which she had removed when he was called away, and which she had kept warm on the hotplate standing on the sideboard. He said casually as he picked up his knife and fork,

'Have I missed anything? There seems to be an atmosphere of restraint between you two.'

Restraint! That was the understatement of the year, thought Julie, and the mildest.

Yet she said, marvelling at the steadiness of her voice, 'You haven't missed anything of importance, Chris. Your mother and I were just—chatting.'

He smiled faintly, his dark eyes perceptive.

'Chatting? What about, might I ask?'

'It's none of your business,' snapped his mother. 'You don't have to know everything!'

'I don't have to,' he agreed without pause, 'but I like to know all that goes on in my home. Julie, what were you and Mother talking about?' Was he troubled? Julie suspected he was, knew he regretted the necessity of leaving her alone with his mother after the promise he had made.

Mrs Dardanis shot her a warning glance that plainly said she had much to gain by keeping the knowledge from Chris that a deal could be agreed to whereby Julie would become rich.

'It really was nothing, Chris,' she assured him with a sudden smile. 'In any case, I've only been here a few seconds—' She stopped as his perceptive eyes flickered to the empty shell of the grapefruit.

'I see . . .' Without further questions he concentrated on his meal, and Julie knew for sure he would later make her speak out. This he did, just as soon as they were alone, his mother having gone out immediately she had finished her breakfast. She would not be in until dinner time, she told them.

'So you weren't interested in this magnificent offer my mother made you?' Chris was watching Julie closely after hearing of the conversation which had passed between the two at breakfast.

'Of course not,' she answered derisively. 'I wouldn't have been interested even if I had been your—your—pillow-friend. But as for its being a magnificent offer,' she went on reflectively, 'she didn't mention any specific amount—just that she would pay me five years' allowance money.' Somehow, in retrospect, the whole thing seemed funny and Julie found herself laughing. 'I wonder how she'd have reacted if I'd said you paid me ten thousand pounds a month?'

A smile of sheer amusement curved the finely-chiselled mouth.

'She'd have concluded that either I had become weak in the head, or that you were something extraordinarily special in bed.'

'Oh—you!' Julie's amusement died beneath the sudden and overwhelming embarrassment she experienced. She put up her hands to cup burning cheeks. 'Need you be so blunt?' she managed quiveringly at last, and Chris gave a gust of laughter.

'Sorry, child,' he said without any sign of contrition. 'What shall I do to compensate you for what you've had to put up with?'

'Make me a firm promise never to leave me alone with her again,' was Julie's prompt rejoinder, and this time Chris's voice had a serious ring as he made the promise.

'It was just unfortunate this time,' he went on, frowning slightly. Then he paused in thought before adding, 'Still, it has given me an indication of just how far my mother will go.'

'It's a pity you yourself can't break off the engagement.'

He shook his head, and reminded her of all he had previously said.

'Apart from the fact of the promise to my father, in Greece a betrothal is considered binding, is in effect the marriage almost, and often couples live together immediately they're engaged, and it's not unusual, in the villages, for the couple to have two or three children before the actual marriage takes place.' He looked at her and again shook his head. 'So you can see that it is impossible for me to break the engagement.'

'But you're hoping *she* will. She might not, you know,' Julie pointed out.

'You think she is bound just as strongly? No, she can break it if she has a strong enough excuse. My having you in my home should be a strong enough excuse—I'm hoping it will be.' Chris paused ruefully. 'Androula will never give *me* an excuse for breaking the engagement; she has set her heart on the marriage even though she knows I don't love her any more than she loves me.'

'Then why on earth doesn't she forget the

whole thing?' asked Julie with some impatience. 'It doesn't make an atom of sense to me.'

'Not to you, Julie,' he readily agreed, but went on to remind her that apart from the actual engagement, there was the promise made to a dying man, that man being Chris's own father.

'But you were only twelve years old.'

'When the marriage was arranged, yes, but not when I made the promise. I made that to ease Father's mind, to let him die happy.'

She looked at him, at the strong features reminiscent of the valiant Greek warriors of old whose stone statues adorned the museums of the world, at the firm chin and mouth, the jaw thrust out, denoting arrogance and good breeding. She could imagine his wanting to make his father happy in his last few hours on this earth—yes, no matter what the subsequent cost might be.

Androula? How foolish she was, determined to marry a man who did not love her. And it wasn't as if she couldn't get anyone else; Chris had said she was pretty and could have been married long ago. Perhaps her father was entirely to blame, for as Chris had maintained, Greek girls always obeyed their parents, and that was why the custom of arranged marriages still existed in some regions despite the rebellions taking place in the larger towns, and often after the young people had travelled abroad, or been to university and learned much about the way other people managed their lives, independent of parental control and domination.

Julie said thoughtfully, 'I wonder how long it will take now that I'm here, supposedly living with you?'

'That remains an unanswerable question.' He looked directly at her. 'Naturally I want the whole miserable business terminated, yet I can't say with honesty that I'll be glad to see you leave here. In any case, your own situation would be uncomfortable, to say the least, were you to return to England just now.' His gaze held the invitation to confide, but she glanced away to the grandeur of the view across the Square and over to the mighty lift of the Acropolis, its magnificent buildings golden and mellow in the sunshine, and for a few seconds her dreams were in the past when processions weaved and curved through the Propylaea and up to the Parthenon, with its lines of perfect purity dominating the entire rocky platform and, indeed, all the country around. Grand

and noble times, those of ancient Greece, the land which had given civilisation to the Western world. Julie, already intrigued by the history and the mythology, had no wish at all to leave . . . so long as she was safe, not only from the temptations which might result from her living here with Chris, but from her own mounting desires, her growing feelings for him, which she dared not probe to any depth. He was too devastatingly attractive, with that charm, the mastery, and above all, his knowledge of women and what kind of finesse it takes to melt them. He spelled danger and disillusionment, heartbreak and regret.

So she ought to be cautiously telling herself she would welcome an early settlement between him and Androula . . . but it was quite the contrary. She told herself it was her situation with her husband which made her want the delay, but in her secret heart she admitted there were other aspects as well.

A sigh escaped her and she saw him frown. He took her hand in his and she quivered at its gentle warmth as it enclosed her fingers.

'Do not worry if you are disinclined to tell me about yourself and those six years,

Julie. One day, perhaps, you'll feel you can confide. Meanwhile, let us be happy together. I'll take you to my home on the island of Cos just as soon as my business commitments allow. And I haven't forgotten that you want to work in the office. In fact,' he added, glancing at his watch, 'I can take you along with me now. I've a meeting at eleven, but if we go now I can introduce you to Stavros, who is in charge of the main office, and see what he can find for you.'

She brightened then, and felt even better when Stavros was genuinely glad to have her in the office.

'We haf two peoples off this week,' he said to Chris. 'This lady come at very good time, *ochi!*'

'Stavros will make sure you have the correspondence relating to our British firms,' smiled Chris, seeing her eyes dart to a desk where the letters waiting for signature were all in Greek. 'What time will she be finishing?' he enquired of Stavros, and the older man shrugged his shoulders. Julie realised that he had guessed she was no ordinary applicant for a job in the office.

'Whatever time you say, Mr Christos.' The man's black eyes examined her openly, then darted to Chris as if to learn something from his expression as he, too, focused his attention on Julie. He said casually, 'I'll be leaving at about half past four, so be ready. I'm sorry I can't take you to lunch, but lunch is arranged to follow on after the meeting, so business will continue through it.'

The day went swiftly for Julie; she was content to be doing something useful while at the same time occupying her mind to the exclusion of the problems which repeatedly crept into her thoughts when she had nothing to do.

Chris came into the office at three o'clock and spent the next hour and a half on the telephone. He was giving Copeland's another large order, he told Julie when they were in his car on their way back to the flat.

'When I go back they ought to pay me some commission,' she commented jokingly when he told her the size of the order and what it was worth.

'When you go back . . .' Chris's voice was faintly harsh, she thought, and she turned to regard him in profile. His face was set and stern, his mouth rather tight.

'Is something wrong?' she asked curiously. 'You look sort of—vexed—or angry.'

He flicked her a glance, then returned his

attention to the road. It was packed with traffic and Julie thought it was a miracle that there were no accidents.

'I'm not angry, but you do know I'm not eager for you to go back.'

'I meant—later, much later.'

To her surprise there was an abrupt change of subject.

'I've been looking through my work and I feel pretty sure we can go to Cos the week after next,' he told her. 'We'll stay for a few days, maybe a week.'

'That'll be lovely.' Julie was enthusiastic even while being alive to the dangers. Had there been the remotest possibility of Chris's becoming really interested in her, for other things besides anything physical that attracted him, she knew she would be thrilled to be going with him to the island of Cos. She had no illusions about her own feelings, or her determined endeavour not to become too attracted to a man who, she felt, was as unreachable as the stars. 'Shall we fly or go by boat?'

'We'll fly. The ferry takes about eighteen hours. You'll enjoy Cos.'

She knew she would . . . with Chris. But his willingness to take her created a sense of puzzlement, since she knew his work was demanding. She said tentatively,

'Is the trip rather in the way of a reward for what I'm doing—pretending to be your pillow-friend, I mean?' The way the phrase rolled off her tongue without embarrassment amazed her. Obviously she was becoming used to the idea of her assumed role.

'Call it that if you like,' was his noncommittal and surprising reply, and somehow Julie knew she must not probe further.

It was much later when, dressed in an ankle-length black velvet skirt and white lacy blouse, Julie came into the dining-room to put a small flower arrangement on the table. She had bought it in her lunch hour, at the florists just along from where she worked. Chris came into the room as she was seeking for the best place; she looked up at him and smiled. His expression was a mask and she wondered if her action was regarded as a liberty.

'Do you mind?' she asked a little timidly. 'I saw this and loved it.' She held it in her hand as the silence stretched. 'I thought it would add something to the table.'

He spoke at last, his eyes having roamed

over her lovely figure before settling on her face.

'A touch of romance, perhaps?' He was smiling suddenly and her fears dissolved. 'It's pretty. Where will you put it?'

A touch of romance . . . Julie would not have expected the stern and sober Christos to murmur words like those.

'In the centre?' She placed it there, then looked at him for approval.

'Charming.' He was close and before she could guess at his intention she was in his arms, his lips seeking hers. He whispered, 'Put your arms around me,' and she obeyed without knowing why she was letting herself be ordered. Then she saw his mother, in the other room but staring through the arched aperture into the dining-room. So this was for effect, a show put on convincingly for his mother's benefit. 'Darling,' he said aloud, 'you become more and more attractive as the years pass. You and I, my love, will be together until we're old—' Then he drew away, smiling nevertheless, and with no sign of assumed embarrassment at being seen by his mother.

She came forward, her mouth so tight it was no more than a thin line in a coldly handsome face. The brown eyes looked black as pitch, and they glittered. Fury was the woman's only emotion at this moment, and it seemed to consume her so strongly that speech was impossible. Chris said lightly, 'Hello, Mother. Did you have a nice day?'

'Do you have to make love to this girl at dinner-time? Can't either of you wait till you're in bed?'

Julie's cheeks flamed—in fact, her whole body seemed to ignite.

'*Matera*,' chided Chris in tones so calm that Julie was both staggered and indignant. She would have expected him to put his mother in her place. 'Where are your manners? Julie is used to respect—'

'Respect—From whom?'

'Our friends in England. I hope you too will come to treat her with respect, since I think so much of her.'

Sudden fear replaced the fury in Mrs Dardanis's eyes.

'Christos, you'd never think of marrying this woman?'

'I'm betrothed to Androula, remember,' he said in a quiet voice. 'No, Julie and I are content to be as we are. It's a permanent arrangement, so even if I do marry Androula, I shall never give Julie up.' He added before she could speak, 'And now we

113

shall change the subject. What can I get you to drink, Mother?'

'Brandy!'

'Julie—your usual, a dry sherry?'

'Yes, please.' She was watching his mother, saw her hands clenching and unclenching, evidence of a strong emotion being kept partly under control.

'Petros wants to see you,' said Mrs Dardanis coldly. 'I spoke with him today.'

'Tell him to come for dinner any time he's in Athens. He'll bring Androula, I expect. He doesn't travel far without his daughter.'

'He rarely comes to Athens,' she snapped. 'He wants you over in Cos.'

Cos? Julie gave a start and shot Chris a glance. His eyes were veiled.

'I shall be there in a couple of weeks' time. I've promised to show Julie the island and my home,' he said.

'She's never seen it?' slowly and with a curious glance in Julie's direction.

'I believe you are well aware that up till now Julie has lived in England.'

The woman was nodding slowly, her brow thoughtful.

'But now you decide she must live here.' Undoubtedly there was a certain inflection in the tone which, though unfathomable, troubled Julie, and she shot a glance at Chris to discover his reaction, but as always in circumstances like these his expression became mask-like. He said, smiling slightly, 'Shall we change the subject? Can I say how much I like your dress, Mother?'

So suave! thought Julie, so adept at veering the line of conversation if he disliked the way it was running. His mother merely sent him a glowering look, and as soon as dinner was over she rose from her chair, said she would be staying for another few days, tossed her napkin on the table and left the room, closing the door with rather more noise than was necessary. Julie sighed, and a frown creased her brow.

'Chris, don't you care that this rift is likely to go very deep?' She wanted to mention Petros Perides, but for some reason she was hesitant.

'My mother and I have never been close, Julie. She's of the generation where parents are all-powerful, dictators of their children's destinies; she'll never change, never begin to understand that marriage has anything to do with love. To her, it's a state convenient both to man and woman. They complement each other in various ways, but love is never a necessity.'

'Do they never fall in love—the victims of these arranged marriages, I mean?'

'Victims,' he murmured, for the moment diverted. 'A fitting description.' He sent her an amused glance, then went on, 'Yes, quite often couples fall in love after marriage, but more often they never fall in love; they tolerate one another and invariably have lovers.'

'The women too?' Julie queried in some surprise.

He nodded.

'The women too. It's now accepted.' He paused, frowning. 'And it's sad.'

'You obviously believe in marrying for love?' She had no idea why she said that, because from the first it had been evident that Chris did not believe in loveless marriages.

'It ought to be the basis on which a couple form an alliance,' he returned. 'I thought I'd made it plain,' he added, and she nodded at once.

'Yes, you did.' She felt flat all at once, but brightened when Chris began talking about the coming visit to Cos. She was eager to explore some of the famous antiquities, to stand where the Sanctuary of Asclepius looked down on to a breathtaking view of the countryside—the plain abundantly dotted with cypress trees, the Strait of Halicarnassus, and farther out to the shores of Asia. She also looked forward to seeing Chris's real home, the home where his roots seemed to be. He had told her his sisters lived there . . .

And so did Petros Perides and his daughter . . .

'The real reason for this trip is so that I can be shown off to everyone concerned. It isn't a reward for anything I've done.'

He merely shrugged and said casually, 'I'd hoped they'd all come over to Athens—my sisters quite often do, but I now feel it is best to introduce you to them all; it will make our relationship more solid—in their eyes, that is.'

Julie was silent for a moment and then, 'I know I agreed to all this, but I'm going to feel dreadfully embarrassed at being branded a—a—'

'Don't say it!' he snapped, astounding her by the sudden anger darkening his brow. 'Try to remember you're merely acting a part, just as if you were a real actress used to a stage—'

'I'm not a real actress!' she shot at him, 'any more than I was a trained model. Yet I'm expected to excel at both!'

'You've done very well at both up till now,' was his maddeningly cool reply. 'So why the panic—or the show of temper?'

'I don't know how I came to get myself entangled in all this intrigue,' she complained. 'I wish I'd given more thought to the matter of coming here at all.'

'It was a necessity for you to get away,' he reminded her gently. 'You've admitted it, remember.'

Julie nodded resignedly.

'I only hope,' she just had to say, 'that I don't let you down and they'll all guess it's a ploy.'

'You won't let me down, my dear,' was his confident rejoinder. 'You're the kind of person who never does let people down.'

'Androula and her father—you didn't say, when you offered to take me to Cos, that they lived there.'

'Julie,' he returned with a touch of asperity, 'you knew from the first that you'd be required to meet them, so why this attitude of complaint?'

She sighed with impatience and merely replied, 'I sincerely hope all this proves to be profitable. But I have my doubts; it wouldn't surprise me if Androula refuses to break the engagement.'

'It wouldn't?' Chris was frowning heavily as he stared at her, and she wished she knew what his thoughts really were, because his whole attention was on her. At last he said, 'I'm optimistic, nevertheless.'

'Any particular reason?'

At that he smiled faintly.

'I can't see any girl marrying a man who has a pillow-friend as beautiful as you, my dear.'

Chapter Six

The villa stood on a small hill overlooking a fertile plain where citrus fruits and vines flourished, and where pretty gardens shone with a galaxy of brilliance in the afternoon sunshine.

'It's all so beautiful,' breathed Julie, suddenly a little dazed by the fact that she was here, on this spectacular island, birthplace of Hippocrates, the world's greatest physician of antiquity.

'I'm glad you like it.' Chris was smiling down at her as they stood on the patio.

They had just eaten the sandwiches and drunk the coffee provided by Katrina, Chris's housekeeper, after arriving at his home following the flight from Athens.

'You were sure I'd like it.' She smiled as she spoke. 'The house, the view, the gardens . . . everything is just perfect.'

He regarded her with an odd expression.

'Could you live here?' he asked unexpectedly, and she stared at him in puzzlement.

'That's a strange question. I shall never have the chance of living here, shall I?'

He turned from her then, and she wondered what kind of expression he was hiding from her.

'I think we both want to go to our rooms,' he said casually at length. 'I expect you want to unpack and then freshen up.'

She nodded.

'What time do you have dinner?' she asked.

'Eight, usually.'

'I'll go for a long walk, then, after I've unpacked. I'd love to explore—that wood looks interesting.'

'You'll find an abundance of wild flowers.'

She hesitated.

'Androula . . . When shall I be meeting her?'

'I fully expect she and her father will be here in the morning. Mother will have let Petros know we're here.'

'It'll be an ordeal, Chris,' Julie said worriedly.

'I'm aware of it, and don't think I'm ungrateful for what you are doing for me.' He moved so that he was close enough to take hold of her shoulders. She quivered at the warm contact, and as she lifted her face she knew he would kiss her. Expectancy tensed her nerves and sent feathery ripples along her spine. This man was too dangerous, possessing this magnetism which she could not resist. His lips were warm and moist, gentle at first, then hard and demanding, passionately masterful. She felt weak, and because of it she tried to protest when his hand moved to touch her breast.

'Chris . . . please . . .'

'Please, what?' faint mockery in the tone and a half-smile on his lips.

'I said I wasn't being a party to—to—'

'Julie, my dear, why don't you relax, let yourself go?' He kissed her again, this time with increasing passion that attacked the faint barrier of her resistance and she was compelled to respond, arching her slender body, shaping it to his; and came the awareness of his need, and with it her own compulsion to satisfy it. 'Let us go to your room,' he whispered hoarsely. 'Life is for living; we know we attract one another—'

'No!' With a strength she did not know she possessed Julie managed to free herself and made for the door. 'I'm not being your mistress, Chris! Don't tempt me like this or I shall go home!' Tears were close, because of her desire for him, and because of the sure knowledge that if he managed to get his way with her he would consider her as no better than the rest, those others his mother had spoken of. She had wanted him to make love to her, but . . .

'Home?' he frowned. 'You've said that is impossible.'

'Not impossible,' she corrected, her hand on the doorknob. 'It would—inconvenience me, but rather that than the shame I would feel if I sank to the level of those other women you've known.' She was calm now, her expression giving nothing away. 'I'm going for my walk,' she added before he could speak. 'I'll unpack later.'

'Shall I walk with you?' he asked unexpectedly, but she shook her head at once.

'I'd rather be alone,' and she went out before he could comment.

What ought she to do? she was asking herself a few minutes later as she crossed the smooth green lawn towards a neat pathway leading to the wood beyond the periphery of the garden proper. Her mind was deeply troubled; she had no wish to return home and be persecuted by her husband, but on the other hand she was acutely aware of the dangers of remaining in Greece, living under the roof of a man whose temptations she was becoming helpless to resist.

She was also troubled about meeting Petros Perides and his daughter, wondering if they would treat her with the same scorn and contempt as Mrs Dardanis had done. And his sisters . . . But it was to transpire that they had gone to Athens and so the meeting was postponed.

'Still,' Julie murmured aloud as she entered the wood, 'I did know what was expected of me when I agreed to this deception. And at the time it seemed the answer to a prayer, to come to Greece, right away from Mark.'

A deep sigh escaped her, but once within the green and peaceful forest glade she became instantly relaxed and able to appreciate the masses of colourful wild flowers, and on some trees she noticed exquisite orchids growing. There had been a shower and she found herself inhaling the fresh clean smell of rain. Could she live here? Chris had asked—a most strange question, that—a totally superfluous one, she thought, still puzzled as to why it should ever have been asked.

'Feel better?' The casual enquiry was put to Julie when she reached the patio where Chris was sitting on a lounger, clad only in shorts and sandals. He had been reading, but he put the book down as she approached. She had not yet changed and suddenly she felt travel-stained, untidy, for the breeze had done things to her hair. She lifted a hand automatically to brush away a lock that had fallen on to her forehead. Chris smiled faintly at the action and she felt awkward, wanting to get away from him and those all-examining eyes that so often disconcerted her. He said softly, 'I asked you a question, Julie.'

She came forward and stood some little distance from him, looking out over the plain.

'I'm more—relaxed, yes,' she admitted.

'But not happy?'

She swung around to face him.

'The fault lies entirely with you,' she accused. 'You don't keep to our bargain.'

'I wasn't aware we had made a bargain— What I mean,' he went on swiftly as she attempted to interrupt, 'is that there was nothing in the pact forbidding me to appreciate your exquisite beauty.'

She coloured, naturally, and the moment became charged with tension as they looked into one another's eyes and Julie was admitting that he was making a concerted effort to conquer what he would term her inhibitions.

'I'll go and unpack,' she decided in a flat tone of voice. 'And I'll be down later, for dinner.'

He rose as she made a move to leave him, and she was brought close to him with a little tug which she knew she could very well have avoided. He took her face in his hand, then gave a small exclamation of surprise and said with a sudden frown, 'There's no necessity for tears, Julie. Am I such an ogre that I frighten you?'

'Not an ogre—' She managed a thin smile, her eyes moving to the strong brown fingers curled around her wrist. 'A man bent on tempting me to do something I'll regret for the rest of my life.' She lifted the tear-misted eyes and added quiveringly, 'There's no future for me in becoming your bedmate, Chris.'

'But we're living in realistic times,' he returned reasonably. 'The old idea of a woman saving herself for the man she'll marry is as dead as the dodo and you know it.'

'I might know it, but there's no reason why I should automatically agree with it,' she countered, freeing herself from his hold.

He said after a small and half frowning silence, 'Won't you open up to me about those six years, Julie?'

'One day, perhaps.'

'Not perhaps,' he argued. 'When the time suits you it will all be revealed—oh, yes, I'm sure I will have the whole story eventually, but I'd rather have it now.' He came close again, staring challengingly down into her eyes. She was suddenly wavering, on the brink of a full revelation of what those six years had held for her.

And yet, for some reason she was not at this time willing to analyse, she was most reluctant to let Chris know she was married.

If only she had divorced Mark after that first occasion of his infidelity. She would be free now. Yet what would such freedom benefit her? True, Chris found her profoundly attractive, but there was nothing in his manner to encourage her to think that he might be considering a more permanent relationship than the one he was so optimistically hoping for.

These musings led quite naturally to the question: did she want a more permanent relationship with Chris? Did she want to be his wife?

She continued to look up into the bronzed and classical face . . . and without any surprise she knew that she could fall in love with him if ever he should give her reason to believe he cared.

He spoke at last into the silence, to ask again if she would confide in him, but she shook her head.

'One day,' she repeated, and he gave a sharp exclamation of asperity.

'You're a tantalising little wretch,' he said slowly, tawny eyes glinting. 'I've a good mind to do some investigating next time I'm in England.' She looked startled and his eyes narrowed. 'So I scare you, eh? Well, the remedy's in your own hands: you can come out with it right now.'

Somehow his persistence made her laugh;

she received a little shake and then his mouth was hungrily claiming hers, his hands a warm temptation as they slid right down her back to come to rest cupping her curves.

'It—it's time we were changing . . .' Her words faltered, because already she was being aroused—oh, how easily this man could make her want him! 'Chris . . . you aren't being fair!'

'All is fair in love . . .' he quoted, bending his head to claim her lips again. 'This reserve, these inhibitions—' He leant away and shook his head in a gesture of admonishment. 'What's wrong with you, Julie?'

Suddenly her temper flared.

'Because I won't become your lover you believe there's something wrong with me! It so happens, Chris, that I possess, even in these so-called enlightened times, a certain amount of self-respect. Do you suppose I shall throw that away simply to pander to your ego! You've failed, for once in your life, to have a woman just where you want her—at your feet!' She swung away, half fearing he would not allow her to escape. But she reached the french window without hindrance and there she turned. 'I've already threatened to go home if you don't keep strictly to the arrangements, the conditions under which I agreed to come here.'

'So I've failed . . .'

Julie heard no more as she hurried away, into the living-room behind the patio, but she felt instinctively that Chris was laughing at her protests . . . laughing triumphantly.

Drat the man! And damnation to his attempts to bring her to his way of thinking! She had a will of her own; she had ideals.

In any case, she was a married woman . . .

Strange, she never thought of herself as married these days—well, not tied; yes, that was a better description of her feelings. She was not tied any longer to the man who had let her down, and who would have continued to let her down had she given him another chance, the chance he had begged for.

Chris was, as always, immaculate when later Julie came down, having had to wait quite a while by the mirror, endeavouring to collect herself because the very thought of meeting him again gave her tingles of apprehension even while she vehemently declared to herself that she had nothing to be scared of; he wouldn't do anything so drastic that she would pack up and leave him immediately.

His slow smile greeted her; his eyes were alive with amusement. She breathed freely, lifted her head and said with a sort of cool affability, 'Am I late? I took longer than I expected.' She swept right into the room, her dress flowing in a cloud of tulle around her. 'If so, I apologise.'

Chris laughed and would have caught her to him, but she was too quick, taking possession of a deep armchair immediately he began to move. His laugh came louder.

'So cool and collected. I admire your sangfroid. No, my dear, you're not late— and you know it.' His amused eyes stayed on her disconcertingly for a few seconds before he added, in the same tone of amused satire, 'And if you took longer than you expected then it was worth every moment. You look superb . . . and sort of fragile, so that I'm afraid to touch you.'

He was laughing at her all right! But she was able to say with a tilt of her head, 'I'm glad to hear it, though I'm surprised. And now, Chris, shall we have our aperitifs?'

'You know,' he responded musingly, 'no woman has ever been quite so free with me as you. I am beginning to wonder if our attitude towards one another has some deep and significant meaning.' He was now at the cabinet, meeting her gaze through the mirror of the open lid.

'What meaning can it have?' She was aware of quivering nerves, of a feeling of expectation as if he were about to reveal something to her—something pleasant.

'We're—close, somehow.' He swung round on his toes, light as a jungle cat. 'We're intimate without being intimate, if you know what I mean?' Again he was amused; he held her glass in his hand but made no immediate move to bring it to her. 'Do you know what I mean, Julie?'

She was tense now, almost afraid to answer; because she did know what he meant.

'I—I think you're saying there's something between us that has—has nothing to do with your wanting me—physically.' She was flushed, her eyes lowered.

'*Our* wanting *each other* physically,' he corrected without sparing her. 'The attraction isn't one-sided, Julie. Be honest and admit it.'

'I believe I already have admitted it.'

Chris gave her a drink and turned to pour his own; she listened to the tinkle of glass against bottle and in the background was

the whirr of cicadas on the balmy air flowing through the open window. Night had
fallen swiftly; the moon was high, sur-
rounded by stars.

'Yes, I believe we have something else
besides the normal attraction of two people
who like each other,' Chris mused softly.

She sipped her drink, then put the glass
on the table at her elbow.

'Perhaps you're imagining things.' It
sounded weak, and she was not surprised to
hear him say in some amusement,

'Raising a barrier of caution, are you?
Julie, you are not honest with yourself,
haven't been from the first.' He took a drink.
'However, we will not tease ourselves just
now. Dinner will be served shortly, and I
suggest we take our drinks outside for a few
minutes.'

It was a warm zephyr of a breeze that met
Julie, and caressed her face as she took the
chair Chris had pulled out for her on the
flower-scented patio. To the east of the main
garden was the *perivoli*, where oranges and
other citrus fruits hung amid the bright
leaves, like lanterns when they caught the
sun, but now the trees in shadow were neb-
ulous dark shapes, as were the more gaunt
and ancient olives—trees of romantic redo-

lence, hiding events and dramas of the past, enfolding deep secrets within their foliage of silver. Chris broke gently into her thoughts to ask what she was thinking about.

'You look so solemn . . . and so far away,' he added, and she looked across at him with a ready smile on her lips.

'I was thinking of the olives, and the tales they could tell. They're so old, and gnarled, but I love them. They make me feel safe and secure—' She broke off, shrugging ruefully. 'I don't expect you to understand,' she went on presently. 'And don't ask me to explain, because I can't.'

'I do understand,' he answered, surprising her. 'There is a certain stability about the ancient olive tree that reminds me of the English oak. That, too, can hide secrets.'

'Of Cavaliers and Roundheads,' she laughed.

He nodded, but was silent. Julie stared at the strong features, feeling instinctively the vitality of the man. It was shown in the angularity of the jaw, the alertness of the dark eyes. Suddenly she felt weak, as if defeated by some overwhelming onslaught from which there was never to be an opportunity of escape.

Just what had happened to her on that

fateful day when she made her decision to come out to Greece with him? Yes, this attraction had begun then, this inexplicable magnetism which, if she were not careful, would take her further than it was safe to go.

The silence stretched; it was companionable, rather cosy, she thought, and a little access of happiness swept over her, bringing a glow to her eyes. Chris, noticing her change of expression, seemed fascinated, yet he soon glanced away, as if he would not wish her to see his expression.

Phivos, the manservant who was the equivalent of a butler, knocked and opened the door of the room behind. He came to the patio to say dinner was ready.

'*Efharisto.*' Chris's tone was gracious; Phivos smiled and withdrew.

It was during dinner that Julie said, voicing what had been on her mind all day, 'I'm dreading tomorrow and the meeting with Androula and her father.'

'I shall be there,' Chris reminded her.

'Yes, I know—' She shook her head. 'I'll be glad when it's over. It isn't pleasant, being branded a no-good.'

'You've already said as much; but you

have also said you knew what was before you when you made your decision.'

Julie nodded.

'I guess I'm not as thick-skinned as I'd like to be,' she returned unsteadily. 'I'll be scarlet the whole time.'

'Nonsense,' he laughed, then he became serious. 'You won't be convincing if you act the little innocent, Julie.'

'I guess not.'

'And it is imperative that you are convincing. Petros Perides mustn't become suspicious and begin wondering if there's some trickery going on.'

'Is he likely to? I mean, is he extra perceptive?' Julie asked.

The question seemed to amuse him.

'He wouldn't need to be extra perceptive if you were blushing all the while and looking uncomfortable. Pillow-friends are usually proud of their—er—occupations.'

'Chris—don't!'

He only laughed, but she sensed an anxiety about him which made her resolve to carry off the deception in such a way as to soon allay that anxiety.

Phivos appeared and the dessert plates were cleared away.

'*Parakaló sérvire ton kafé stó salóni,*' said Phivos.

'*Né.*'

'Phivos will serve the coffee in the living-room,' explained Chris with a smile. 'We'll listen to some music.'

'I'd like that.'

As they rose he reached for Julie's hand. She felt weak again, and very vulnerable.

But there seemed to be a certain safety in listening to music.

Chapter Seven

Androula stood there, tall and beautiful, a Greek *kore* who would catch the eye of any man. Her raven hair was long about her shoulders, her eyes deep pools of mystery. She had the figure of a model and her voice, faintly alien, was low and musical, unlike that of her father, whose tone was harsh and clipped as he said, glowering at the man he expected to become his son-in-law, 'I want to know the meaning of this—' He swung a furious hand in Julie's direction. 'As I've just told you, your *matera* telephoned me to say—' Again he stopped as if he could find no words to express what was in his mind.

He had called at the villa without phoning, but Chris had known he would come and he and Julie had been waiting for him. Androula drove the car along the drive to the villa and right up to the front door. She alighted, and Julie, watching from the living-room window, gasped even then, having to admire the beauty of the girl's movements even before she had the opportunity of seeing her face properly.

And Julie was now trying to find an explanation why Chris had not fallen madly in love with the girl.

He had declared she could have married had she wanted to, and Julie thought she was so lovely she could have had any man she set her sights upon. She plainly wanted Chris, although there was nothing to reveal this in her manner, or in the looks she sent him every time he spoke.

'If my mother phoned you,' Chris said calmly, 'then I expect there's little I can add to what she said.'

'You are disrespectful to your parent!' Petros Perides' eyes glinted. 'Your *matera* doesn't gossip!' His accent was more pronounced as his voice rose. 'She just told me what you are doing—bringing your pillow-friend to live with you! What about your betrothal to my daughter?'

'I have not broken it,' Chris returned in the same calm and controlled tone of voice. 'But I have known Julie for several years. We've established the kind of relationship which cannot be severed. I expect my mother told you this?'

Petros made no answer.

'You will give her up!' he ordered, and this time it was to Chris's eyes that the dangerous glint came.

'I seem unable to make myself clear either to you or to my mother,' he said, and now impatience edged his voice. 'Julie and I will remain friends even if I marry Androula.' He turned to her. 'You will understand, won't you?' he said, and now a certain gentleness softened his tone.

She shrugged elegant shoulders. She seemed dulled by resignation as she replied, 'Of course, Christos. Women in Greece know their husbands have pillow-friends. It is accepted—' She looked at her father and added, though a little falteringly, 'It is not unusual, Father. If you remember, you had—'

'Quiet, child!' He glowered at her. 'I will not accept this woman—'

138

'You are not being asked to accept her,' cut in Chris stonily. 'And her name is Julie; you will please speak of her with respect.' He seemed, paradoxically, both furious and sympathetic as his eyes strayed for a fleeting moment to the Greek girl who, having declined his invitation to sit down, was still standing regally erect, her small hands clasped in front of her in an attitude of submission, and Julie's heart went out to her because she was unable to launch herself out, away from the restrictions imposed by a domineering father whose stronger will had obviously controlled hers throughout her life.

Julie wondered if she would like to break free, but then realised the girl had no qualifications which would assist her to find a job. No, with girls like Androula marriage was still the only solution to her finding some kind of niche in life.

'Respect!' spat out Petros, glaring at Chris as if he would dearly like to strike him. 'What respect do such women ever get in Greece?'

'I think you can manage without my presence.' Julie was stiff with temper, and it was mainly directed at Chris for putting her in this situation. Yet underneath the anger was

139

the understanding that this scene, like the one with his mother, had to be necessary if everyone were to be convinced of what Chris was trying to put over to them: that come what may he intended keeping Julie as his mistress.

And poor Androula was ready and willing to accept that.

'We are getting nowhere!' Petros had merely sent Julie a contemptuous glance when she spoke, and now his attention was again with Chris. 'Your *matera* and I decided to get on with arrangements for the marriage. It will take place within the next two or three weeks!'

Suddenly a smile appeared, to rob Chris's mouth of its severity.

'A wedding without a bridegroom wouldn't serve much purpose,' he said, not without a glance of apology in Androula's direction. 'I am not yet ready to marry you,' he told her gently. 'You will have to wait a little longer, my dear.' He spoke softly to her, but it was plain that he meant what he said. It was also plain that his attitude was more in the nature of an acquaintance than that of a man who was betrothed to the girl. But Julie recalled his saying that he and

Androula had never once been alone to-gether.

'The promise you made to your father?' Petros threw out the challenge in a much quieter voice than before, and his very dark eyes fixed those of Chris as if he would dare him to treat this matter lightly. 'You have not forgotten it?'

The ghost of a smile curved Chris's lips. He seemed tired by this interview—or maybe bored, mused Julie as she made her way towards the open window leading to the patio.

'It is scarcely likely that I could ever for-get it, Petros, for it has caused me a great deal of anxiety over the years. I sometimes wonder, had I my time over again, if I would have made it.'

That was honest enough, thought Julie as, unobtrusively, she stepped out on to the patio and moved away from the disturbing eyes of Androula which had been on her for most of the time. Perhaps—and it was natu-ral—she was wondering how Chris could prefer a woman so much less beautiful.

Julie strolled away from the house, her thoughts naturally erratic as she tried to sort out exactly what would happen now. It seemed that neither Petros nor Mrs Dardanis would agree to a broken engagement, and certainly Androula would never voluntarily break it. A solemn promise supported by a church service had by Greek law bound the two together, and she would consider it a sin to go against the law.

It did seem that things were not going to be as simple as Chris had so optimistically surmised.

On reaching the periphery of the garden Julie stopped, feeling she must know what had transpired. She swung around; the car was still there, so the argument was continuing. A sigh escaped her as she opened a little gate and went through into the wild part of the villa grounds. A woodland path took her into an area where nature had been allowed to run riot, and she was surprised to find treasures which also grew in her own country, flowers like campions and fox-gloves, and an abundance of Erica thriving beneath pencil-slim cypresses and plane trees. It was peaceful here, away from strife, away from people and all the problems, both petty and serious, which intruded so often into their lives.

'Life is what you make it . . .' Not much real truth in that saying, she thought grimly as she stooped to caress a lovely blue campanula from which a delicately-coloured butterfly had flown. No, life was so often affected by what others did to you, and sometimes even unimportant encounters could create unforeseen disturbances in your life.

She little knew, as she eventually threw off these mind wanderings, just how much trouble one particular encounter was to give her.

'So nothing is settled.' Julie was with Chris, half an hour after Petros and his daughter had left. 'It's all been for nothing if Androula is willing for you to keep your—friend.' She managed not to blush, but Chris smiled just the same, sensing her discomfiture.

A sigh escaped him as he answered, 'It's incredible, and different from what I expected. Androula's had a good education and she is also a highly intelligent young woman, so it has often puzzled me why she hasn't broken away from her father. Had she been in your country she would certainly have gained her independence long before now.'

Julie nodded in agreement.

'Yes. Parents would never dream of holding on to the reins so long. But even if they wanted to their children would be brave enough to break away and make lives of their own. A parent doesn't own you body and soul just because you have his blood in your veins.'

'The trouble with Androula is that she hasn't anyone to confide in, to talk to,' Chris explained. 'Her mother died when she was very young and although she has aunts and cousins she knows they'd never help her to leave her father—on the contrary, if she dared to confide in any one of them that she wanted to leave home they would immediately tell her father and she'd find herself in serious trouble.'

'Does she have any money? But she can't, seeing that she's never gone out to work.'

'As a matter of fact, she has a small fortune left her by her mother.' He stopped rather suddenly and a wry grimace changed his expression. 'Don't forget that the dowry custom was strong at the time Androula and I were pledged to one another by our parents. My father was just as interested in the dowry which would come to me along with my bride as any other parent. It was to have been quite substantial.'

Julie looked at him long and hard from her chair opposite to his on the sunlit patio.

'Chris,' she said at last, 'with such a beautiful girl, and a dowry that was substantial—why are you so averse to marrying Androula? She's so lovely, and gentle—' Julie shook her head. 'I can't understand you.'

He was silent for a space as if words were difficult—which was not like him at all. He was usually ready with an answer, being as confident and self-possessed as he was.

'For one thing,' he said at last, rather slowly. 'I am not the kind of man to be dictated to, and from the moment Petros and my mother began badgering me I dug in my heels; it was a natural reaction any man worth his salt would have felt. The other thing is—' He stopped and the look he sent her set her pulses racing. 'The other thing is, Julie, that most men, even Greeks quite often, do look for something deeper than surface beauty in the woman they will have to spend the rest of their life with.' He spoke quietly and somehow there was an undercurrent Julie would love to have fathomed. She said with a dawning frown,

'How do you know there's no real depth to Androula? She seems a very sincere person to me, a girl with a lot to give besides a lovely face and figure.' She was staring at

145

him, her eyes wide and serious; she was finding herself troubled about a girl she scarcely knew, a foreign girl who ought not to be her concern in any way whatsoever.

'I haven't really come to know Androula,' admitted Chris wryly and with a thoughtful frown knitting his brows. 'And the only reason is my aversion to the dictatorship of our parents. I might have fallen in love with her if we'd been left alone to sort out our destiny for ourselves.'

'It's a logical argument, Chris—' She paused, then added, 'Why don't you try—I mean, make an effort to get to know her?'

'You would like me to do that?' The question seemed pointed and Julie had to look away. She was ready to admit to herself that she would not in any way be happy to see Chris falling in love with Androula.

'I don't know . . .' She shook her head. 'I suppose it's too late now. You seem determined not to marry her.'

'I am,' grimly and with an injected harshness to his voice which Julie did not like at all. 'Let's change the subject, shall we?' he said abruptly. 'Would you like me to take you to the Asclepeion?'

'Of course.' But she was still frowning. 'About Androula, Chris. You say she has money of her own. Can she get at it? I mean, is it controlled by her father?'

'I wouldn't know—and I am becoming bored by the whole weary business. We won't discuss it any more.' Although his tone was repressive Julie was, by some spur, wanting to know more about the girl and this money she had.

'You can't just dismiss the matter,' she told him reasonably. 'However, it's about Androula as an independent person that I'm talking now. If she has money of her own then she can break away, surely? You said yourself that it's puzzled you why she's allowing herself to be dominated by her father, that she ought to break away.'

'I did say something of the sort, but I also said there isn't anyone to whom she can turn. She wouldn't go off by herself without some encouragement from someone; she'd feel too alone. You have to remember she has been under the constant protection of her father up till now, and habit is difficult to throw off.'

'But you think that if she had someone to help her, to rely on, she would make an effort to break away?'

Chris looked puzzled.

'What's this all about, Julie? You appear

to be disproportionately interested in Androula.'

'She—sort of—troubles me,' returned Julie with a puckering of her forehead. 'I like her, very much, so I sympathise with her if she wants to break away.'

'It doesn't seem that she does want to break away.' His tone was as puzzled as his gaze as he waited for her to respond.

'You can't be sure of that. Oh, I know it seems on the surface that she wants to marry you, but has it ever occurred to you that her main reason could be the desire to get away from her father's domination?'

'No, it hasn't ever struck me that way at all.'

'It wouldn't be the first time a child has married only in order to escape from the influence of parents who are too possessive or autocratic.'

'Perhaps,' he agreed, lifting a hand to suppress a yawn, 'you are right. However, I said we shall change the subject. Let us make plans for the trip to the Asclepeion. When would you care to go?'

It was arranged they should go the following day, but the eagerness which Julie displayed did not in any way overshadow her concern about Androula. In fact, she could not get the girl's plight off her mind, no matter how hard she tried.

'If only I could help her—or just talk at first, to see what she really wants, Chris—or is it simply her freedom?'

Julie spoke to herself as she sat in her bedroom sewing, shortening a dress she had bought in Athens. It was a cool cotton with bright poppies on a lime green background. Dramatic, the boutique assistant had said, and Julie had plunged, paying more for a summer dress than ever before, but she knew she would look good in it, and she intended wearing it for the trip to the Sanctuary of the God of Healing, an Asclepeion built after the death of Hippocrates, the father of medicine who followed the ideas of Asclepeios that a beautiful setting, fresh air, good food and cleanliness were the first essentials of maintaining good health.

Even as she strolled among columns and climbed a mountain of steps Julie was plagued by thoughts of Androula. But she felt reluctant to broach the subject to Chris, although she did want to get some ideas as to how Androula could be helped.

But first the girl's wishes must be discovered, since, strange as it might seem, it could be possible that Androula was in fact content to be domineered by her father.

The day following the visit to the Asclepeion Chris had to fly back to Athens, just for a meeting, so Julie had the day to herself. With only a few moments of indecision she phoned Petros Perides' number, praying that it would be his daughter who answered; and it was. So far so good. But how to begin? Julie decided there was no profit in prevarication, so she came straight to the point, saying she would like to talk to Androula in private.

'Is there somewhere where we could meet?' she added, speaking urgently because she was afraid Petros would come upon his daughter and demand to know who she was speaking to.

'Yes—er—is it important?' The voice was almost timid, and Julie flinched at this lack of self-confidence. The girl's personality was being smothered.

'It is, Androula,' she answered quickly. 'Can you come to the *cafeneion* in town?' As soon as she said that Julie realised it would not be prudent at all to meet there where so many eyes would be turned upon them, curious eyes whose owners could just be the instrument of Petros's getting to know of the meeting between the two girls.

'Well, it's a public place,' began Androula, at once revealing her own fear.

'I can see that now. You can't come here, obviously, because although Chris is away in Athens, there are the servants.' Julie thought for a second or two and then suggested they meet in a small park to the north of the town. 'It should be private enough there,' she added, and as Androula agreed, a time was arranged.

Julie was there promptly. Androula was ten minutes late, as her father had been cleaning the car. She had said she was going to the hairdresser and had an appointment, but Petros had merely decided the hairdresser could wait.

'So I can't stay long with you,' Androula added, 'I must go to the hairdresser; my father will notice if I haven't been.'

How awful to be so crushed, frowned Julie, again taking in the beauty of the girl, the classical features which might have belonged to the goddess Athene herself. 'What is it you want to see me about? If you are willing to give Chris up—

'It isn't that, Androula.' Julie saw a fallen tree and suggested they sit down. 'I was puzzled about you,' she went on without preamble once they were seated. 'Have you never thought of breaking away from your father?'

The girl looked slantways at her.

'You were puzzled? But why should you bother about me? We don't know each other.'

'It worried me, the situation. I don't mean as regards Chris and your engagement to him. I mean—well, I began to wonder if marriage to Chris meant freedom from your father.' She looked steadily at her, half turning her head. 'I don't believe you're in love with him, Androula.'

'But you are,' from the girl with a promptness that startled Julie and left her floundering for words.

But it was soon borne in upon her that Androula wasn't saying anything extraordinary after all, simply because, as she, Julie, was supposed to have been Chris's girl-friend for several years, it was only logical for Androula to conclude she was in love with him. But the girl's declaration had startled her . . . and made her realise that her feelings for Chris would have to be analysed before very long. The physical draw could be the basis for something deeper . . . but she was still married, had not even begun divorce proceedings.

She said with a little shrug of resignation, 'You were bound to reach that conclusion, Androula.'

'But Chris—I cannot believe he loves you, because he is not the kind of man to bother about such things. Yet he will not give you up—' The Greek girl stopped and shook her head, and Julie noticed with dismay that tears had dampened her lashes. 'The truth is plain, isn't it? He doesn't want to marry me and that's why he brought you to Greece, so that we could all see you and know that a pillow-friend existed. He felt sure I would give him up, but I c-can't—!' She put her face between her hands and for a long moment the sound of her weeping was all that broke the silence. Julie moved close to her and placed a hand upon her shoulder.

'You need a friend,' she said softly. 'A friend who will help you.'

'To do what?' Androula had glanced up swiftly. 'You know! You have guessed that I want to get away from my father—Oh, what have I said? You will tell Chris, and he will tell my father. I shall be in such trouble—!'

'I have no intention of telling Chris or anyone else,' Julie broke in. 'You've just realised that I want to be your friend, so why should I let you down?'

'I don't know what I'm saying.' Androula dried her eyes and blew her nose before putting the handkerchief away into her pocket. She looked small and helpless, yet she possessed a certain dignity which should serve her in good stead if she did make a bid for freedom.

'You were only wanting to marry Chris in order to free yourself from the yoke put on you by your father.' Half statement, half question; Julie knew the answer, of course, but waited for Androula to voice it.

'Yes, you have guessed it all. Oh, Julie, what can I do?'

'You want to marry for love?'

'Of course.'

'You must have had chances,' Julie suggested.

'My father has always been determined to force me into marriage with Christos, so any admirer was sent away,' Androula explained.

'You've never even been out with a boyfriend?' It was unbelievable, Julie thought, seething with anger at the sheer injustice of the situation.

'Never—I haven't even been alone with

Christos. Perhaps I would have fallen in love with him if I had.'

'Yes, that is possible.'

Androula looked mistily at her.

'He'll never marry you, and it is a shame, because you are so nice. He will never marry me either, and I—I don't know what is going to become of me!'

'You must consider breaking free.' There, it was out, and the startled expression which Julie expected was there on Androula's face, but strangely there was no fear, nor any instant reaction in the negative. Let it sink in, decided Julie, who had thoughtfully brought a flask of coffee. She went to the car to fetch it, smiling at the look of gratitude that came to Androula's eyes.

'What the doctor ordered,' smiled Julie as she handed her the cup. 'There's sugar if you want it.'

'No, thank you.' Androula sipped the hot coffee and became thoughtful. 'Chris lets you have his car. You are favoured.'

'It's the small one. He has two here on Cos.'

'And one in Athens. I have never been in any of his cars.'

'The engagement was like a sham, wasn't it?' asked Julie gently.

Androula nodded her head.

'Yes, but it was binding—and still is, according to my father. But we both want to be free.'

'Then all you have to do is tell Chris, isn't it?'

'No! I want to get away from my father, and if it has to be marriage to Christos—'

'Androula, I've intimated my willingness to help you. I want to be your friend. You're not a child but a mature woman with a will and mind of her own. You know you can't go on for the rest of your life being totally controlled by another human being, whoever it might happen to be. I know you have money of your own, so the major difficulty doesn't even exist.' Julie paused, but Androula's interest was strongly caught and she seemed eagerly waiting for Julie to continue. 'There's no reason, Androula, why you shouldn't live on your own, in an apartment. You can begin mixing with people, and you'd obviously meet someone very special—No, please don't interrupt. You're very beautiful, Androula; I mean it. You can have your pick, so why be cowed by your father into waiting for a man who you say will never marry you? How long are you

156

going to wait, and remain single? Surely you want a family?'

'Every Greek girl wants several babies. But, Julie, I think—I think I'd b-be scared of leaving my father.'

'It's a big step, I admit, and it will be a period of trauma when you do leave, but I can guarantee that within a few weeks you will be glad you were brave enough to do what you want, and not be a prisoner—yes, you are virtually imprisoned, Androula, and your father is your gaoler.' Julie felt somewhat apprehensive at the way she was trying to persuade the girl to leave home, yet she knew she could not ignore her plight; it was as if some compulsion over which she had no control were urging her to offer help in a practical way. 'I'll find you an apartment if you want me to,' she went on when Androula still remained silent, her expression unreadable. 'Chris and I will be back in Athens next week, so I can look around. Once settled, you can then change the accommodation if you want, but it seems to me that it's imperative that you get away just as soon as you can.'

To her surprise Androula was nodding; she looked excited, eager to accept the help offered, but Julie feared that once she was home she would falter and then abandon any idea she at present had in her head.

'It sounds wonderful! Oh, Julie, will it work? I mean, suppose my father tried to get me back?'

'He has no power over you; you're of age, your own mistress entirely. Do this thing,' she begged earnestly. 'Make the break and be free!'

Androula looked at her in some perplexity.

'I can't understand why you are doing this for me, Julie.'

'Nor can I give you a reason,' came the immediate admission. 'I only know I pity you, know you could be happily married with a home and husband like any other woman. You're wasting all the precious years of your youth—on what? Tell me, Androula, on what?'

'I have no answer, Julie, to that question. I know you are right in saying I am wasting my life, my youth—in fact,' she added tragically and with a sudden lump in her throat, 'my youth has gone already.' At which Julie had to laugh, heartily.

'What rubbish! You've got all the very best years of your life before you, but only if you make a break, at once.'

'I'll do it!' In her excitement Androula jerked the cup and the coffee spilled on her dress. 'Oh . . .'

'I'll see to it.' Julie's handkerchief was out and she dabbed at the stain until it was almost dry and scarcely noticeable.

'I don't know why I've been so lucky in meeting you! And to think I was ready to hate you when my father mentioned you to me after Christos's mother had phoned. Can we be friends for always?'

Julie smiled a little wryly and just had to ask, 'You want to be friends with my kind of person?'

'I don't care what you are: I really like you, because you're kind and you care about people. What have morals to do with it?'

Julie said after a slight pause, 'One day, Androula, you'll know more than is on the surface—and then I'm sure you won't regret becoming my friend.'

They fell silent drinking their coffee. Julie took the empty cup presently as Androula glanced at her watch and gave a frightened little start.

'Time you were making for the hairdressers, Androula. You're sure they can do your hair?'

'Yes, I'm sure they'll fit me in; I'm a

regular client, you see.' She rose as she spoke and together they walked over to where their cars were parked, just outside the railings. Julie put the flask and cups away in the basket she had brought and the girls said goodbye after arranging for Androula to send a note by a maid she could trust.

'You have someone you can fully trust?' asked Julie.

'Sophia, yes. She knows my situation, and although she would never be familiar she often shows her sympathy in various ways. I am sure I can trust her with the note.'

'You won't change your mind?'

Androula shook her head.

'No, for you have convinced me that it is wasting my life to go on like this—' She shook her head strongly. 'I will not weaken, Julie, have no fear of that.'

And, looking into those steadfast dark eyes, Julie felt the doubt melting away. Unless something drastic happened, Androula would soon be free.

Chapter Eight

The note arrived the following morning when Sophia, aware of the secrecy, put it

160

under a cushion on a chair in the summer-house. Julie had not expected it so soon but had gone to the summerhouse just in case. She was jubilant as she read.

'I have definitely made up my mind. Will you please find me an apartment as soon as you are back in Athens? I will make sure Chris never learns of your part in all this, Julie, but I do hope we can find a way of seeing each other as I shall need you at first, until I become used to managing my own affairs. I wait eagerly for you to say you have found me a place to live.' Androula had gone on to say she would make out a cheque in Julie's name if she would like this. Julie rang later, ready to put the phone down at once should it be Petros who answered. But it was Androula.

'I'm so glad you didn't change your mind,' began Julie after being assured that Petros was out walking and would not be back for at least half an hour.

'You feared I would?' Androula's voice quavered a bit, as if even talking about her decision made her a little afraid. Julie could understand perfectly just what the girl was going through in resolving to break away from her father after so many years of domination.

'I wasn't quite sure, but almost,' she added quickly. 'You seemed firmly resolved when we parted.'

'I suppose it was because I said I'd send you a note. You felt I was hesitating?'

'In a way, yes. But on the other hand you did seem sure you knew what you wanted and were determined to get it.' Julie paused and added sincerely, 'I think you're a very brave girl, Androula. It must be an anxious time for you, but believe me, in a few weeks you'll be glad you had the courage to do it.'

'I know. It's just the time in between. I keep thinking how terrible it would be for me if my father found out what I intended doing.'

'He won't know a thing until you're away.'

'But I'll have to send him my address, and he will surely come to try to make me go back home.'

'Don't be in too much of a hurry to give him your address,' advised Julie at once. 'Let him know you're safe, of course, but give yourself time to settle into your own home, and that interval will also give your father time to realise he no longer has jurisdiction over your life.'

'Yes, that is a good idea.' There was a

small pause and then, 'I'll just have to wait now until you get in touch. My father usually takes a walk about this time every day, so it will be safe for you to phone me.'

'I'll begin looking around just as soon as we get back to Athens,' promised Julie. 'You'll want a furnished place at first?'

'You advise that?'

'Of course, so that you can move straight in.' She did not want Androula to be harassed by fixing up an empty flat. She was determined to make the move as smooth as was possible so that the girl could settle in peacefully.

'I'll leave it all to you—And, Julie, I shall be grateful all my life—'

'Androula, I'm doing this because I want to, because to me there is gross injustice in your father's attitude.'

'No one has ever bothered about my plight before,' said Androula brokenly.

Julie sensed she was close to tears and decided to ring off, which she did after assuring the girl once more that she would soon find her an apartment and she would be around when she moved in.

Julie was thoughtful throughout lunch, so

it was not surprising that Chris should enquire if anything were wrong.

'No, nothing.' But she went on immediately, 'How long are we staying on Cos?'

His eyes flickered.

'You want to leave?'

'I—er—well, I thought you might be wanting to get back—er—your work . . .'

'Julie,' he said slowly while his eyes never left her face, 'something is wrong. You've enthused repeatedly about the island, and the house, but suddenly you want to return to Athens. What is the reason?'

She had coloured. Her pulses had quickened as she thought of the real seriousness of what she was contemplating. Chris would be furious with her—yet he would probably have to know sometime that she had been instrumental in the break between father and daughter. Chris would call her meddlesome, which was true in a way; she was meddling in something which was none of her business. Yet she seemed to be driven by a compulsion she could neither explain nor control. She wanted Androula to be happy, to find a wonderful man and live a normal life.

'You're imagining things, Chris,' she began, but he instantly interrupted her.

'It's very plain that you are uncomfortable,' he said rather sternly. 'Come out with it. What makes you want to return to Athens?'

Julie suddenly thought of an idea.

'To tell the truth,' she explained, 'I don't like being so close to Petros Perides. I could bump into him and—well, I'd feel ashamed.' She managed to look straight at him while telling the lie. 'That's the only reason, Chris, and I hope you'll understand.'

He seemed faintly puzzled, but she was relieved to hear him say, 'If you really feel that way—yes, we'll go back to Athens.' But he added with a frown. 'This is my main home, Julie, and I like to be here as much as I can. Necessity keeps me in the capital, but I prefer Cos.'

She nodded.

'I understand we must come here at times, and I shall have to get used to it.' She stopped because it occurred to her that once Androula moved she would then break the engagement and Julie's presence would no longer be necessary.

So in saving Androula from her father's domination she was shortening her own time in Greece. And once she was back in England Mark would probably begin persecuting her again.

A sigh escaped her, and it brought the question, 'What was that for? You puzzle me, Julie. I wish I knew more about you.'

She looked at him, saw him push his plate away as if he was no longer hungry.

'You will, Chris,' she promised. 'I shall tell you everything about those six years quite soon now.'

'Soon?' He looked questioningly at her. 'Any particular reason why it will be soon?'

She said rather tiredly, 'Please don't question me, Chris. I can't be open with you at present, so bear with me.' Something in her tone touched him deeply and he reached across the table to cover her hand with his.

'I won't question you, my dear. Don't look so strained. You worry me.'

'I do?' she felt warm all at once, and happy. 'I really worry you?'

'If you are not happy, yes, of course you do. I brought you here and I care about your welfare.'

Was that all? He felt an obligation towards her? Well, what else had she expected?

A thin smile touched her lips.

'It's nice of you to care,' was all she could find to say, and he frowned again.

'Nice is a weak and uninteresting adjective. "Thoughtful" could be more appropriate. I do think a lot about you, Julie, often pondering on that six-year gap in your life which you keep so secret.'

'It seems important to you that I disclose everything.'

'I feel sure it would do you good to unburden yourself. Secrets can lie heavily on one's mind.' He paused and smiled encouragingly at her, smiled in a way that set her pulses racing. 'There's much common sense in the saying that troubles shared are troubles halved.'

Julie nodded in agreement and for an indecisive moment she felt tempted to confide. Yet conversely she felt the old reluctance not to let him know she was a married woman. She feared his whole attitude towards her would change, that he would be cool, reserved, keeping her at arms' length.

And she knew the very last thing she wanted was to be kept at arms' length . . .

She shook her head, and saw his impatience even before she spoke.

'Not yet, Chris, it isn't the right time.'

He shrugged and reached automatically for a bread roll.

'Have it your own way!' he almost

snapped, and from then on they ate in silence.

Julie was delighted with the apartment she had found for Androula; she paid the first month's rent from her own pocket, then phoned through to Cos. It happened to be Petros who answered, and she promptly returned the receiver to its rest. He could not have taken his customary walk today, she thought with some vexation, and hoped the same thing would not happen tomorrow.

Meanwhile Chris was busy at his office, but was concerned about Julie.

'You're sure you are happy, working at a typewriter all day?' he asked.

'It isn't all day, as you know. I finish at three in the afternoons, so I have plenty of time to look around the city.' She sent him a smile and added, 'In fact, I enjoy getting to know my way about—the street names and squares. And I've been to the Acropolis a couple of times.'

'As long as you aren't bored, Julie, I'm content.' His fine eyes were fixed to hers; she wished she could read what was behind his expression. For the first time she was asking herself if he found in her more than the physical attraction which he so openly admitted. The future . . . if he cared . . . if he wanted to marry her.

She said into the silence, 'I could never be bored in this city—no one could.'

'I'll take you out to dinner this evening,' Chris told her. 'We'll dine in the Plaka.'

Chris took her to the Attikon, where he was known, so they were provided with a table right at the front, facing the raised dais which served as a stage for the dancers who would be performing for the diners. It was rather noisy, being frequented by Greeks rather than tourists, but Julie liked the atmosphere, the feeling she was one of the 'locals'. She came in for smiles, and stares that stripped—but she was used to this by now, this undisguised probing by Greek men which had so disconcerted her at first.

They began with fish, caught that day and grilled with lemon and parsley, with a cucumber side salad and crusty rolls. Lamb followed—'baby lamb', as it was always called wherever one ordered it—with vegetables and a rosé wine to accompany it. The dancers performed to the music from an orchestra composed of violin, clarinet, lute and *santouri*, the dance which intrigued Julie being the *tsakonikos* which, Chris explained, was much like the crane dance which was based on the escape of Theseus from the Labyrinth at Knossos, on the island of Crete. The men held each other tightly by the arm as if striving not to lose one another. The steps consisted of a series of serpentine figures representing the winding passages of the Labyrinth.

'You don't often see this particular dance nowadays,' whispered Chris while it was still in progress, and Julie's fascinated gaze fixed on the youths who danced with incredible agility as they made repeated labyrinthine convolutions with tireless perfection. 'Old-fashioned people, especially sailors, do keep up the *tsakonikos* in various parts of Greece.'

'It was . . . wonderful,' breathed Julie when it was ended. 'I love the Greek dances!'

'You can learn, you know.'

Yes, but how much time do I have? she asked herself. Aloud she said, 'Not many women do the dances, though.'

'Like all other customs, those concerning dancing are changing. You will see women quite often, and they dance alongside the men—something unheard of at one time when all Greek girls had to be chaste, having no contact with men until their wedding night.'

'Terrible!' she declared, frowning. 'Thank goodness the light is beginning to dawn!'

He laughed.

'Nevertheless, girls never leave the parental home until marriage.'

'Never?' she echoed rather sharply. 'Surely you're wrong, Chris?'

His brows lifted in surprise at her tone.

'I should have said, rarely.' He paused a moment, staring at her across the table. 'You seem to feel strongly about it.'

She shrugged carelessly.

'It was just a thought. I mean, it seemed strange that a girl could never free herself from the parental yoke.'

'Custom again. She has to be protected, remember. There are too many womanisers about, and a girl who left home might find herself in the kind of trouble that would disgrace her for life and make marriage impossible. You see,' he went on with a sudden frown, 'it is still a disgrace, a stigma, even, if a Greek girl has an affair before marriage.'

Julie fell silent, troubled about Androula. Suppose she met one of these womanisers? Suppose she was lonely and sought the wrong kind of company? She had been so closely protected that she would probably fall into the first trap set for her.

By the time they were back at the flat Julie was almost ready to abandon the idea of helping Androula. But she had to admit that allied to this thought was the idea of her own self-preservation. In other words, she wanted to stay with Chris . . . stay for ever . . .

Immediately they arrived back at the flat Julie declared her intention of going to bed, but Chris dismissed this idea with the abruptly-spoken words, 'It's only half past ten. You won't sleep.'

'You want me to stay with you for a while?'

'I'm going for a walk and I'd like you to be with me.'

No mistaking his eagerness for her company . . . but what was his ultimate objective? She had already established the fact that he wanted to have an affair with her, and she had also admitted to the danger she was in, that his magnetism drew her far too swiftly to the point of no return just whenever he decided to use that devastating charm he possessed, and which had affected her right from the start, she now admitted. She had felt she disliked him intensely during those hours when his hard eyes had been so critical even while there were no signs that he regarded her as anything more than the model who had been forced to parade before him.

'I'll go up and tidy myself,' she said, 'and then we'll go for the walk.'

'Good girl.' His dark eyes roved her body and she coloured when they rested on the firm round breasts before moving lower, in a sort of slow enjoyment, before reaching the slim ankles and lifting again to her face.

Their stroll took them across the Square and on to a road of busy traffic but which led to a quieter one where white houses, tall and elegant, were framed by plane trees and cypresses.

'It isn't like Cos,' sighed Julie, speaking almost to herself. 'That was really beautiful.'

'Yet you were in a hurry to leave it,' he was swift to remind her. She said nothing to that and he went on after a moment, 'I am still somewhat puzzled about the reason you gave me. It didn't sound convincing at the time, and it sounds even less convincing now.'

She slid him an oblique glance, profoundly

aware of the hint of suspicion that had accompanied his words.

'It worried me that I'd bump into Petros.'

'So you said.' His voice was cool, urbane. 'And I said it didn't sound convincing.'

'If you were in my position, branded the mistress of—' She was halted by the crack of laughter which broke into her indignant words.

'Now how on earth could I be in a position like that?' he demanded, still laughing.

Julie's chin went up.

'It isn't a joke!'

'You knew what was expected of you.'

'True, but that didn't automatically make me immune to a feeling of shame!'

Chris stopped abruptly and caught her hand.

'You know, Julie, you're rather sweet,' he said, and promptly kissed her full on the lips.

'Oh . . .' She was all confusion, the words 'rather sweet' echoing in her ears. Did he really mean it, or was it the kind of 'softener' a man of his experience would employ? She said at last, 'You're always saying I puzzle you, but sometimes you puzzle me. I never quite know how to take the compliments you pay me.'

'So naïve—and I like you for it.' To her surprise he bent to kiss her again, and his arm slid about her waist. She felt the warmth of his body as he pressed it close and a little access of sheer rapture shot through her. 'For your peace of mind, my dear, all compliments are sincere.'

'But leading to—what?' she just had to ask, and he gave her a little shake.

'Always suspecting me of ulterior motives,' he chided. 'Why are you forever on the defensive?'

'Perhaps because I have to be,' she replied on a challenging note. 'You've already made it clear that you'd like the sham situation we're in to become a real one.'

'Of course. I find you so attractive that I want to make love to you. You should be flattered.'

Julie had to laugh.

'And what kind of a compliment is that supposed to be?'

'Another perfectly genuine one.' He began to walk on again and she fell into step beside him, happy that he had retained his hold on her hand.

She was silent for a space, then changed the subject, asking why he had not seemed put out by the stalemate situation concerning him and Androula.

'It'll sort itself out.' His tone had a note of carelessness about it that induced Julie to say,

'You're not too perturbed that Androula hasn't acted according to your plan and broken the engagement.'

He was a moment or two before he spoke and she had the impression that he had been weighing up his words.

'The situation has changed, somewhat. I'm not quite so eager now for the engagement to be broken.'

'Not—!' She caught her breath, knowing as she did that as soon as Androula had shaken off the restrictions of her father she would tell Chris she no longer wanted to marry him. She might even confess that the only reason why she had wanted marriage was to escape from her father. 'But—but all this has been a waste of time—my coming here, I mean.'

'You think so?' briefly and with a strangely cryptic inflection.

'It would seem like it.' She paused, uneasy and perplexed. 'Are you saying you might decide to marry Androula, after all?' Perhaps, she thought, this was the time for telling him the whole truth and letting him learn that he didn't really have a chance of marrying the girl to whom he was at present engaged. Of course, Julie soon thought better of that idea, and in any case he was speaking, to say quite emphatically that he had no intention of marrying her.

'Yet you don't want the engagement broken—? Chris, you're being maddeningly secretive!'

'Which,' he countered with a sideways glance, 'makes two of us. Perhaps when you open up I might be encouraged to do the same. However,' he continued more briskly, 'let's change the subject. I want you to meet my sisters, so I'm inviting them and their husbands to dinner one evening next week.'

Julie was silent, and they walked along for some time before the silence was broken; it was Chris who spoke.

'You're not happy?'

'I know you said I'd have to meet them, but . . .'

'I shall be there to sustain you.' His voice carried a thread of amusement that annoyed her out of all proportion.

'I ought never to have agreed to your absurd plan!' she seethed, knowing full well she didn't mean a word of it. 'It's so humiliating to pose as your—your—oh, you know what!'

'Let's turn back,' he suggested mildly. 'I find no pleasure in walking out with a young lady who loses her temper for nothing.'

'Nothing?' she exploded. 'You were laughing at me!'

'I was amused, yes, but certainly not laughing in the way you are implying. We shall go back and you can go to bed. Perhaps by the morning you'll be in a better mood.'

'A more tractable one, you mean!'

'Certainly a more obliging one,' was his cold response. 'As I have reminded you several times, you knew, before you consented to join me in this plan, what it entailed.'

Julie said nothing and was angry with herself when tears gathered behind her eyes. Chris had withdrawn his hand; he was hurrying, and had put some distance between them so that she had to trot to keep pace with him.

Once in the elegant sitting-room of his apartment she said goodnight and turned away, towards the door through which they had just entered. Her head was lowered, but suddenly his finger had tilted her chin and he noticed the glistening lashes.

'What is it, Julie?' His voice was a gentle caress, and much to her dismay she began to cry. He took her close in his arms; she nestled against his chest, feeling foolish yet savouring the comfort of his hold and the soothing words he spoke. 'Tell me what's on your mind, dear. I can't have you troubled like this.' So gentle the tone, so tender the caress of his hands as they moved over her back while still holding her tightly against him. She lifted her face; he took the handkerchief which was tightly clasped in her fingers, and dried her eyes and cheeks.

'I'm silly,' she murmured. 'I have no idea what made me cry. I think I'm over-wrought.' A mistake, that word, because his instant reaction was to ask for a reason why she should be overwrought.

'It doesn't require super-intelligence to realise that you have something weighing heavily on your mind. I must know what it is, Julie.'

She sought for something that would satisfy him, but failed. She was under no illusions that what she was doing for Androula was oppressing her just as much as the matter of her being married. She felt she could do without either problem, that she could then be happy. She was having qualms regarding Androula; Chris had thrown her into confusion by saying he wasn't too keen on the engagement's being broken, yet he had also stated quite firmly that he had no intention of marrying the Greek girl.

And there was the nagging worry about Mark, and his importance in her life.

It was no use refusing any longer to ignore the fact of Chris's manner with her. She had been telling herself she was mistaken in cherishing the hope that he might be falling in love with her. But now . . .

This embrace had no trace of passion or desire; it was given purely for comfort, as many of his kisses had been for comfort; she knew that now.

She said quiveringly, 'I'll tell you soon, Chris—tell you everything, I promise, but not yet, not tonight.' She buried her face in his coat, felt him stroke her hair with gentle fingers instead of stiffening at her refusal to confide, as she had fully expected him to.

'Let me get you a drink, dear.' He led her to a chair and pushed her gently into it. Julie watched his lithe frame as he strode over to the cabinet. Dear . . . Twice he had said it within a few minutes. Not 'my dear' which really meant nothing, but dear . . .

He gave her a brandy and looked stern when she grimaced.

'It'll settle your nerves.' He was thoughtful, frowningly so, as if debating something not quite pleasant. 'I ought to take you for a holiday,' he decided at last. 'How about a cruise in the Caribbean?'

She hesitated, thinking of Androula who was waiting to hear from her, hear that an apartment had been found for her.

'That would be lovely,' she agreed, but went on to add, 'it will take a while to arrange, I suppose?'

'Not too long—a week, if we can get a cancellation, and quite often this is possible.' He smiled down at her as she sipped her brandy. 'And while we're away, in a romantic setting like the West Indies, you might be tempted to open up and set my mind at rest.'

Set his mind at rest. That was a strange thing to say.

But she allowed it to pass and when she had finished her drink she rose with the intention of going to bed. But she found herself in his arms, her lips captured by his, and this time ardour flared, and there was a sort of proprietorial manner in the way his hand moved across her throat and down the slope of her shoulder, the fingers moving the neckline so that her flesh was bare. She quivered and pressed close, with no immediate desire to wrench herself away.

Chris said a trifle thickly, 'Put your arms around me,' and she reached up obediently, caressing his nape before thrusting her fingers into his hair. His hands were a warm and rapturous pleasure as they moved slowly along her curves. She quivered when he enclosed her breast, made no protest when, after a little while, he slipped the wide shoulder strap down and she felt the gentle movement of a hand sliding down to caress her before his lips followed, his tongue teasing the nipple, hardening it to a little bud of desire. Julie strained against him, thrilling to the whipcord hardness of his thighs and more shyly aware of his throbbing need of her.

She ought to resist, one part of her mind was saying, but she was honest enough to admit that Chris's magnetism was making her more and more aware of herself as a woman, a woman no longer fulfilled . . . a normal woman who had gradually become sensible of the fact that sex was vitally important . . . and she was missing it.

'Julie,' he whispered close to her ear, 'we

must make love. We need each other—don't deny that you want me, because you'd be lying.'

It was true; she swallowed hard as if the action would provide her with time, and common sense, and the power of resistance.

Resistance . . . ? She was clinging to him; she lifted her face to invite his kiss, and she moved in rhythm with the sudden passion which he made no attempt to control.

It was becoming too late for withdrawal from this situation, and in any case, she had no wish to withdraw. She had gone too far, reached the point of no return.

Yet pressing for attention was the vital fact that Greeks never married their pillow-friends. If she surrendered now there would be no hope of a future with Chris. Was it worth it? She had no proof that even if she resisted he would ever ask her to marry him. And if he did, what would his reaction be to her confession that she was already married? Would he wait until she had gone through the trauma of divorce, or would he decide he didn't want what another man had had first?

'The time is now, Julie,' whispered Chris as if aware of her thoughts. 'This night—let us be together.' His hands were roving her body with gentle strokes and she tingled with a sort of rapturous expectation as the silent entreaty formed on her lips, 'Love me, Chris . . . take me . . .'

She had showered and put on a filmy nightgown and was brushing her hair when she heard Chris softly turning the handle of her bedroom door. She swung around, brush idle in her hand, colour tinting her cheeks. The desire, the erotic flame that craves the moment of fulfilment, the abandonment of doubts . . . all these had vanished as if washed away in the strong spray of the shower. The interval seemed to cool every spark of the primitive fire which had been responsible for her willingness to have Chris come to her room. She noticed he too had showered, but unlike her, he had not bothered to protect his hair and it shone now in the one muted glow from the bedlight, shone with dampness and cleanness and made him seem more attractive than ever.

She gave a deep sigh as he came in and closed the door. His dressing-gown was held by the cord which was loosening against his silken threads. He had nothing on beneath, she realised, and suddenly felt quite faint.

He came towards her slowly, his dark

eyes piercing and perceptive. Yet a half-smile curved his lips and the sardonic inquiry carried an undercurrent of confidence.

'What's wrong? Changed your mind?'

Julie bit her lip, colour increasing in her cheeks.

'I expect we've both cooled off,' she managed, feeling extremely foolish and embarrassed.

'You might have,' he returned slowly, 'but that can soon be rectified.' He took another step, then looked her over. 'You're very beautiful,' he murmured, and reaching out a hand took the brush and placed it on the dressing-table, his dark eyes never leaving her face. He drew her to him, sensing her reluctance but ignoring it. His mouth locked to hers, then moistly explored, caressing her throat, her shoulder, and rested for a long moment on her temple. The warmth of his body seeped through the silk of his gown and the much finer material of her own attire. The sensation of longing began slowly to envelop her, stirring erotic nerves as with a sort of arrogant mastery his lips closed over hers, fanning the flame of desire already smouldering within her. How swiftly he could arouse her! It was frightening, yet at the same time exhilarating as excitement lent strength to her own contribution as she spread her fingers into his hair, a certain sensuality even in its wiry texture against her palm.

'Let's get rid of this' . . . with a dexterous movement Chris had the straps of her nightgown slipping down her arms and the next moment she stood naked before his admiring gaze. She looked up to see a nerve pulsating in his cheek, and eyes smouldering with passion. With a primitive, uncontrolled mastery he drew her fiercely to him, to his naked frame as his dressing-gown slipped to the floor to lie beside the filmy garment already lying there. Julie shuddered against him, tormented by the desire for fulfilment which was aching in her loins. She strained passionately, strained as if she would meld her body irretrievably with his. He laughed softly with triumph as he swung her off her feet and strode over to the bed. The cover had been turned back and he laid her down, then bent to cover both heaving breasts with warm and gentle hands. His fingers captured the nipples and she knew the pleasure-pain of their strength as they pinched until the hardened buds made her writhe with longing for the final act.

But he was intent on love-play and seemed

to delight in her little moans of entreaty, and her every nerve cell was crying out when at last he slid over her to send them both, within seconds, along the heady flight to paradise . . . and beyond.

It was a long while later that she heard him murmur in his sleep, '. . . adorable . . . but what is she hiding?'

Chapter Nine

'What is she hiding . . . ?' The words were ringing in Julie's ears as she woke, coming to her more strongly as she turned to smile tenderly at the sleeping figure of the man who had at last succeeded in his aim: to have her for his own. What was she hiding? It seemed the time had come to tell him everything, yet she felt a reluctance still, not sure of how he would react.

The first words he spoke, as his eyes opened to full wakefulness, vanquished all hesitation, and she knew the time had come for a full confession.

'All that fuss, Julie, and you weren't a virgin after all.' No reproach, merely interest in the faintly-narrowed eyes as he leant up on one elbow to stare directly into her eyes.

She nodded, moistening her lips. Strangely in this momentous instant her mind dwelt on whether she looked dishevelled and she pushed fingers through her hair. He smiled, took her hand and put it to his lips.

'I'm—I'm m-married, Chris.'

It was his turn to nod.

'I felt it must be that.' He sat up, turning his whole body to face her. 'Tell me all about it, Julie. I want nothing left out, understand?' The sternness was out of keeping with the look in his dark eyes, for she saw only tender concern there which encouraged her to tell him everything, even to Mark's attack on her in Angela's flat.

'So that was the reason for your need to get away,' nodded Chris. 'You were very wise.'

She searched his face, not quite able to accept that there was no trace of accusation or anger . . . or disappointment. Her heart caught unexpectedly as it dawned on her that if Chris's interest in her was limited to the physical side, then naturally he would not be at all perturbed by the knowledge that she was a married woman. Fear, a heart-jerking fear spread throughout her mind and body and she cried desperately, 'You don't love me? You don't want to marry me?'

Silence, the kind of silence to make her heart begin to die within her.

He said presently, taking her trembling hand in his, 'My dearest Julie, have I to remind you that it is the man's prerogative to—er—pop the question?'

'Oh . . .' She sagged with relief, then was brisk and a trifle angry. 'You frightened me! How could you—'

'Darling Julie, relax! These moments are trying for you. But one anxiety I shall spare you at once.' He took her in his arms and kissed her. 'Will you marry me when you are free, my darling?'

She gave a shaky laugh and for a long emotional moment was unable to voice a reply. Then quite absurdly she said, 'Androula—have you forgotten her?'

'Not at all,' was his calm rejoinder after he had kissed her lightly on the cheek. 'By the time you are free she will have realised the futility of holding me to my promise, so I, too, shall be free.' He leant away, smiling amusedly as he added, 'Meanwhile, we shall continue to be lovers—'

'But Greek men never marry their pillow-friends—' Again the absurd words fell from her lips, and to her surprise he gave her a little slap.

'We'll not mention that description ever again! You are not in that particular category; you're my wife-to-be. I love and respect you, as I have done from the beginning.' He smiled then and shook his head as a tiny sigh left his lips. 'I've known for a while that I wanted to marry you, and for that reason I didn't tempt you too much—' He broke off and sighed again, resignedly. 'I hadn't the strength to continue resisting you . . . and my own desires and inclinations, and so we're lovers after all. Lovers, Julie, not anything else.'

She snuggled closer, resting her head against his chest, thrilling to the feel of his wiry hair upon her cheek.

'Is it true? Perhaps I'm dreaming and when I wake I shall find you gone.'

'Whenever you wake I shall be here beside you,' was his fervent rejoinder, and she noticed his voice was husky and very low, as if some intense emotion were affecting him. 'For always, my Julie, remember that.'

It was at breakfast that they again spoke of her marriage. Chris decided quite firmly that

Julie should begin divorce proceedings right away.

She agreed, but frowningly suggested there might be complications, with her living abroad.

'No such thing.' He was brisk and businesslike and she felt safe and secure at having someone think for her. 'I'll see my lawyer tomorrow. However, we do have to go to England quite soon, as I've promised Copelands I'll look at some new designs that they've brought out using Indian pure silks.'

Her eyes flickered.

'They sound exciting.'

'To me also. They've begun doing housecoats and leisure wear. I might be interested in those too.'

'And you want me to come with you?'

He smiled at her across the table.

'Of course. You and I will always be together whenever it is possible.'

She warmed to this, but her thoughts flitted quite naturally to the future and she found herself saying, 'Until the family arrives. Then I shall have to be a stay-at-home wife.'

'Only at first. There's nothing wrong with a nanny, you know.' Chris paused a moment and his face softened. 'I expect you still feel the loss of your baby?'

She nodded sadly.

'It's something you never get over—No,' she amended swiftly, 'You do get over it, because time heals. But you never forget. We'll have children, but my baby will always have a place in my heart.' She looked at him rather mistily. 'You wouldn't mind that, would you, Chris?'

His smile was slow and tender.

'I wouldn't want it any other way, my darling. A mother who can forget completely is to my mind somewhat hard, a little unfeeling.'

'Yes, I agree.' For a long moment she was away from him lost in a dream, and he made no attempt to break into what he realised was a sacred little interlude, which would soon pass so that she would come back to him again. His smile was ready and tender when that moment arrived.

'Be happy, my love,' he said simply and, reaching across the table, he laid a gentle hand upon hers.

Julie was to try several times before she managed to get Androula on the telephone.

'What happened?' she asked anxiously. 'I

was beginning to realise that your father would become suspicious if I kept phoning and then ringing off.'

'He's had trouble with his legs, so he hasn't been out walking.' Androula's voice was not quite steady as she went on, 'If he should be ill after I left I would never forgive myself, Julie.'

'Has he had the doctor?' Julie was frowning heavily. Just like the old man to have something wrong with him at a time like this, she thought disgustedly.

'No, and he refuses.'

'Is it serious? He could obviously get to the phone.'

'Perhaps it is not serious.' A slight pause and then, 'Have you found me an apartment, Julie?'

'A most attractive one—'

'In Athens?' Androula's tone gave no indication of eagerness, and Julie's heart began to sink.

'No, not in Athens, but not far away; it's in Old Phaleron, in a road bordered with pine trees and oleanders, and the view extends to the island of Salamis and Aegina. It's well furnished—quite luxuriously, in fact, and I've taken it for three months.'

A silence followed while Julie waited anxiously, feeling it would be a miracle if Androula had not become so scared that she had changed her mind, especially as her father was not too well. But when at last the Greek girl spoke it was to say, though still in a rather shaky voice. 'I wonder how I can move without my father knowing?'

'Does he never leave the house at all?'

'He hasn't done so since this pain has affected his legs.' Anxiety again, which caused Androula's accent to become much more pronounced—in fact, she spoke almost in broken English, so different from the way she usually spoke.

'We'll have to think of something . . .' Julie paused, then just had to ask, 'You haven't changed your mind, Androula?'

'N-no—I've j-just asked you how—how I can bring about the move.'

'You must stay firm,' Julie said, but in a soothing tone of voice. 'As I said, we shall think of a way.' What a pity they couldn't enlist Chris's help, she mused, and did wonder if she dared take him into her confidence now that he and she were to be married. Undoubtedly he would be glad at getting his freedom, but would he be party to deceiving Androula's father?

'I can't think how we are to manage it,'

from the other end of the line. 'Oh, and I forgot to mention that Sophia is willing to come with me if I promise to employ her all the time.'

'That's wonderful news! So you wouldn't be alone. Have you agreed?'

'I said I would. I'd have to, if I let her leave my father's employment, because she would not know what to do—Julie, there are so many troublesome things! I would very much like to have Sophia, but—but supposing I decided to return to my father? He would not take her back, and she is alone in the world but for a cousin somewhere.'

'Alone?' It was must unusual for any Greek not to belong to a very large family, but Julie supposed there were exceptions. 'Well, you can employ her, Androula. She really wants to be with you?'

'Yes, she is most eager. I think that she, too, is tired of being bossed about by my father. Sometimes he is not nice with her.'

'It seems a most excellent arrangement to me.' Julie was racking her brain for some way in which the moving operation could be carried out. 'Is there any way Sophia could get your things off the island?'

'She never leaves Cos.'

'And she has no ideas about moving?'

'She said that if only my father would go away for one day we could manage to get to the airport. But it would mean I would have to leave a lot of my clothes and books behind.'

'It might be worth it, Androula. Later, you can ask your father for them.'

'Yes—I suppose so . . .'

Ignoring the hesitation, Julie asked about Androula's money.

'I am free to draw what I want. My father never thinks I shall leave him until I marry, so he has never made any arrangements to control my money. It was left to me by my mother, you see.'

It surprised Julie that her father had not thought to control the money; but it illustrated his arrogant confidence that he had his daughter completely subjugated, that she would never create a situation where she would need money independent of him.

'Where is your bank account?' July enquired, and was told it was in Cos.

'Then the first and most important thing is to transfer it to Athens.'

'I can do that? How do I do it?'

Julie gave a small sigh, filled once more with misgivings about what she was doing.

Androula did not even know how to go about transferring her money to another bank. How was she going to cope?

Julie bit her lip, almost wishing she could undo what had already been done, but the next moment she was remembering her advice to Androula to remain firm. If the girl was to remain firm then Julie should not begin to dither!

'The thing seems to be to get your father away. But you say he can't walk? Where is he now?'

'Resting on his bed.'

Julie gave an impatient sigh. Why hadn't she thought of these snags before encouraging Androula to leave home? The apartment was rented now, and ready for occupation.

'Leave it to me, Androula,' she said at last, trying to put confidence into her voice. 'When can I be sure of getting you on the phone?'

'Father doesn't get up until about nine o'clock now, so you can phone me about half past eight.'

'There wouldn't be any danger of his hearing you and wanting to know what it's all about?'

'The phone is at the other end of the villa from his bedroom.'

'All right. I'll ring at half past eight to-morrow.'

Although Julie continued to work her brain overtime she failed to think of a safe method of getting Androula away from her father. But as it happened fate was to take a hand indirectly in the form of what—had she known of it previously—Julie would have termed a disaster.

Mark had discovered where she was.

And he arrived at the Athens apartment at the very time when Mrs Dardanis was paying a visit to make another demand that the date for a wedding between her son and Androula be immediately set. Chris was in the very middle of an argument when Mark arrived and, pushing the maid aside, strode into the sitting-room and without preamble demanded to see his wife.

Julie, who had gone to a smaller room to get away from her future mother-in-law, heard the commotion, and her heart turned right over as she recognised her husband's harsh and over-loud voice. She was trembling from head to foot as she made her way slowly from one room, along a short passage, to another. Mark was blustering, and she realised he had been drinking heavily.

Hot and ashamed, she looked at Mrs Dardanis. Their eyes locked; she saw both contempt and triumph in the older woman's eyes.

'So you are this person's husband,' she said slowly, her attention reverting to Mark's figure as he stood aggressively in the middle of the room. 'And you have come to take her home? Do so, then, and at once! She certainly isn't wanted here!'

'Mother—' Chris's voice was surprisingly calm, 'keep out of this. In fact, I'll ask you to leave this room.'

'I have a right to be here! This woman is a—.'

'Do you want me to rid myself of your unwanted presence forcibly?' interrupted her son's almost gentle tones.

'Mark,' quivered Julie, ignoring everything else, 'how did you find me?'

He swung around, to face her as she stood in the open doorway, her cheeks ashen, her legs feeling like rubber, ready to collapse beneath her.

'It wasn't so difficult!' His eyes were bloodshot and glittering. 'I happened to ask enough of the right questions of a sufficient number of people, and managed to get results. *You* talked to *me* of unfaithfulness, yet you're living with this—this foreigner! Living with him! You slut—' He got no further as Chris took him by the shoulder and swung him around. Julie trembled at an expression she had never encountered on Chris's face before. He reminded her of some pagan murderer, a man without a grain of humanity. White with fury, he drew back his clenched hand and would have delivered a knock-out blow if Julie, springing to life with a speed that amazed her, had not flung herself between the two men.

'Chris, don't do it! Just—just get him out of here, but don't do anything that could put you in danger!'

Mrs Dardanis's face was a study of malignant triumph and Julie cursed fate for sending Mark here at this particular time. The older woman said quietly, 'Your mistress is right, Chris. Don't put yourself in danger of the law merely for the absurd defence of a woman you're living with. Let her go back to her husband—where she belongs.'

Chris had released Mark, who staggered back to finish against the low couch and, becoming off balance completely, flopped into the cushions. What a disgusting spectacle! Julie felt too humiliated to remain and she turned to the door. Mrs Dardanis rasped before Julie could go through it, 'Come back here! This party is yours, not ours. Shirking won't do you much good.'

'Mother,' snarled Chris, advancing purposefully towards her, 'get out of here at once—before I throw you out!'

'Chris!' protested Julie, and received a glowering look for her interference.

'I said, get out of here!' Chris's manner must have had some effect on his mother, because although she opened her mouth to make a protest, she changed her mind and went from the room. Julie listened for the front door to close, but no sound came. The woman had not left the apartment.

'And now,' Chris was able to give his full attention to the man sitting there, 'you'll get out, too, and quick! Julie is divorcing you and then she and I will be married.' He spoke with quiet deliberation as if aware that Mark's mind was befuddled by the drink he had consumed before coming here. 'Do I make myself clear?'

Julie was watching him, her fear of a moment ago dispersed as soon as he spoke to Mark of his intention of marrying her. Until then she could not help wondering if this scene would have an adverse affect and that Chris would consider he would be wise to extricate himself from the situation. But it was very plain now that nothing in this world would make him change his mind, and a flood of tenderness brought a light to her eyes which caught his attention and a swift smile took the sternness from his lips. But only momentarily. He was soon giving his attention to Mark again, and although there was much blustering on Mark's part, and threats of violence hurled at his wife, it was Chris's strong and implacable personality that conquered in the end. Mark rose unsteadily from the couch and Chris rang the bell for a servant to show him out.

Chris's parting shot was, 'Remember—I will not hesitate to have you arrested should you molest my fiancée in any way in the future. Understand?'

Mark nodded wordlessly. He seemed to have accepted total defeat, realising no doubt that Julie's champion was not a man to battle against.

'Oh, Chris,' cried Julie when the door had closed, 'I'm so sorry. I'd have done anything to avoid a scene like that.' She brushed a hand across her eyes; she was overwrought and it was with difficulty that she managed to hold back the tears. 'What is your mother thinking? She will never accept me now.'

'You had been hoping she would?' He looked at her in some surprise.

'Eventually, yes, I had hopes of her coming round.'

Chris was shaking his head.

'False hope, darling. My mother is hard, adamant. She will be more optimistic than ever now of persuading me to give you up and marry Androula.'

'She's still here.'

'Yes, I know.' He moved to take Julie in his arms. His kiss was tender, his words soothing to her ragged nerves. 'It's all over, my love. It was unfortunate that he found out where you are, but he won't trouble you again. And the divorce will go through quickly and without a hitch.'

'You're so confident,' she sighed.

'Of course,' calmly and after kissing her again. 'We'll be married before very long, I promise you.'

'I feel—well, not too good, Chris.' Automatically she put a hand to her head which had begun to ache. 'I'll get an aspirin from the bathroom.'

'Yes, do that.' Chris subjected her to a searching and concerned scrutiny. 'It's been one hell of an ordeal, love, but a little rest will work wonders on your nerves. I hope the headache doesn't stop you from sleeping.'

'Sleeping?' she queried.

'You're to have a lie down on the bed—and don't get up until I tell you.'

'But—' She stopped as he gave her a little push.

'Off you go, sweet, while I deal with Mother.'

'It won't be easy.'

'No need of the warning,' he returned with a grimace. His eyes slid to the cocktail cabinet and he added ruefully, 'I'll fortify myself with a drink—in any case, I feel in need of one!'

Julie went through the hall to the far end where the bedrooms were situated, and she halted abruptly on hearing Mrs Dardanis's voice coming from the guest room. She had concluded that the woman was either in the small sitting-room or the dining-room . . . but she was up here, using the telephone. Julie could not help staying where she was because it was plain that the woman was telling someone about the scene which had just taken place. And it was soon obvious that she was speaking to Androula's father.

'So you must come over at once. My son will be ready to throw this creature over and marry your daughter, but only if we strike while the iron is hot, as they say! When can you come—Never mind about your legs! They can't be that bad! In any case, you are able to get into a car and then a plane.' The voice was aggressive and harsh, and not for the first time Julie wondered how a woman like this could have a wonderful son like Chris. Julie was just about to move on when an idea sprang into her mind that caused her to stay and hear more. 'Tuesday? Why not later today—you could get the late afternoon plane—What? Oh, all right! Tomorrow on the half past eleven plane. You should be here by two at the latest, and that's allowing for heavy traffic from the airport to here. I'll stay overnight and be here when you arrive.'

Swiftly Julie made for her bedroom door and was through it before Mrs Dardanis emerged. She closed the door and leant against it, her eyes going to the telephone by the bed. She must phone Androula at once, even at the risk that it might be her father who answered. But to her great relief it was Androula who answered.

'Can you be ready to move tomorrow?' Julie asked without preamble.

'Tomorrow?' fearfully. 'But—but—Father—'

'Will be catching the half past eleven plane for Athens.' Julie went on to explain as swiftly as she could, and promised to be at the airport to meet her off the private plane which Julie said she must arrange to get.

'There are a couple of air taxi firms which I noticed when Chris and I were on the airport at Cos, so try to get one which can leave about a quarter to twelve or perhaps a little later. Having a private plane means you will be able to bring everything with you instead of having to leave some of your belongings behind. As I said, I'll meet you at the airport and have a taxi ready to take you to the apartment. Is Sophia still willing to come with you?'

'Yes, but—.'

'Androula, you still want to be free of your father?'

'Yes—oh, please do not misunderstand me! I am scared, Julie, that is the truth!'

'I wish I could be there with you, but we have only one day that I can be sure of, Androula, as I feel your father will want to return to Cos on the late evening plane to-morrow.'

'Will it be easy to get a private plane?'

Julie sighed, thinking again how little this girl knew, how inexperienced she was in what to most people would be the ordinary things of life.

'It will be easy,' she answered, then advised that Sophia be sent to the airport right now to make the arrangements. 'It would be unwise to use the phone at all,' she said. 'Sophia sounds an intelligent girl and I feel you can trust her to carry out your instructions efficiently.'

'Yes . . .'

'If you allow this opportunity to pass,' Julie warned, 'you might never have another one. It's a miracle, Androula, so take advantage of it.'

'I will—yes, I will do everything you advise, Julie.'

'Good! I must go now, but I shall see you tomorrow. Phone me as soon as your father leaves the house to let me know when the private plane gets in so I can be there in plenty of time.'

'You are sure you can get away?'

'I work in Chris's office—although I had today off because we were going to one of the beaches, but Mrs Dardanis arrived. As I was saying, though, I work in the office, so I shall go as usual in the morning, but then I shall say I feel off colour and leave.'

'Christos, though. Doesn't he work in the office?' queried Androula.

'I expect Mrs Dardanis will arrange it that Chris is home at the time your father is to arrive.'

'Will Christos tell you?'

'I rather think he will keep your father's visit from me, initially. I shall tell Chris that I want to do some shopping when I leave work at—supposedly—four o'clock and that I shan't be home until about six, and I reckon he will welcome that news, because it will give him time to get your father out of the apartment without my seeing him.'

'You feel Christos will keep my father's visit a secret from you.'

'No, not really—but that isn't important, Androula,' Julie said with slight impatience. 'Is everything clear in your mind? You know exactly what you have to do?'

'Yes . . . I think so.'

Julie paused in thought and then, 'I'll give you a number at the office where you can get hold of me before I leave for the airport, but if you do phone you'll have to make sure your father is not about.'

'Of course—I do understand. But it is all coming straight, Julie, in my mind. I understand what you say about this opportunity perhaps being the only one I shall ever get. I'll be there if I can, as you say, hire a private plane.'

'Did you transfer your money to an Athens bank?' Julie thought to ask, and was gratified to hear that Androula had written to the Athens branch of her bank and the transfer was going through.

Julie breathed a sigh of relief. It would seem that in spite of her fluctuations of enthusiasm Androula was gritting her teeth and telling herself that this move had to be made, and Julie was profoundly thankful that the girl had the support of Sophia, whose character appeared to be stronger than that of her mistress.

Julie had faith in Sophia's ability to get the whole operation running smoothly, but nevertheless, she would be glad when she eventually saw the two girls get off the plane and could take them to the apartment.

It was two hours later when Chris came up to the bedroom which they now shared. She

209

had not at first wanted to lie down, but seeing that she had to obey Chris and stay in the room she decided to rest, and soon she had fallen asleep, helped, no doubt, by the effect of the two tablets she had taken.

'How are you, darling?' He stood by the bed staring down at her, tenderness in his dark eyes which caused her heart to jerk with pleasure. 'Feeling better?'

'Much better, thank you.' She sat up, helped by his arm around her back. 'I didn't think I would sleep, but I did.' She could not meet his gaze; she had a dread of giving away this guilt she harboured. If only she could confide . . .

He said into her thoughts, 'Do you want to stay a while?'

She shook her head. 'No. Any time away from you, dearest Chris, is wasted.'

'That is a wonderful thing to say to a man.' He bent and kissed her, and very soon the flame of passion flared between them to a conflagration and they made love with the warmth of the Grecian sun pouring through the window to caress their naked bodies.

'I love you so much,' whispered Chris as the fires died and only smouldering ashes remained. 'My one and only sweetheart.'

'I was afraid, for a short while when Mark was here, that you would change your mind,' Julie conferred.

Chris reached down to give her a little smack.

'Such thoughts deserve chastisement,' he told her with mock severity. 'There will be no changing of minds—either yours or mine. This is for ever, Julie. Surely you know that?'

'Yes, but I really was afraid,' she quivered. 'It was such a dreadful experience for you to go through, one I never contemplated happening.'

'It is over and done with and we shall not speak of it again. I want you to promise me that.'

'I promise,' she whispered huskily, her face buried against his chest.

Chapter Ten

It was later that evening, when they were strolling hand in hand in the gardens below the Acropolis, gardens bright from the illuminated sacred buildings above, that Chris remarked casually, 'I think you should buy a new dress for the dinner party I've invited my sisters and their husbands to. Why not go shopping after you leave the office to-morrow—No, why not leave early to give yourself plenty of time to look around the boutiques and find something special?'

Julie glanced up swiftly, feeling elated at this bonus. It saved her feigning illness so as to leave the office early, and obviated the necessity of warning Chris that she would be late home. As he was sending her shopping himself he would be prepared for her to be late.

She said, feeling specious and guilty at deceiving him, 'Suppose I search around and find nothing to my liking?'

'Then go again the next day. But try to get it. Stay till the shops are closing if necessary; there is no hurry to get back.'

'All right, I'll try.' She did not look at him, knowing as she did that she would have no time for searching around for a dress. She would be too busy helping Androula and Sophia to settle in, and she strongly suspected that Androula would keep her till the very last possible minute.

Julie wondered just when Chris would tell her about Petros's visit. She knew he would tell her some time, knew also that the visit would avail Petros nothing; both his and

Mrs Dardanis's hopes they cherished today would be dashed long before this time tomorrow.

And by this time tomorrow Androula should be free. Julie sent up a little prayer that all would proceed according to plan, that Petros would not be really ill, or Sophia be unable to get the private plane, or that Androula would at the last moment get cold feet—Julie snapped shut these harrowing thoughts and tried to concentrate only on the things that could go *right*.

In any case, when she and Chris returned to the apartment there were other things to think about and to discuss. Chris told her he would prefer to live most of the time on Cos, though the Athens home must be kept so that they could stay when they visited the capital periodically.

'On business mainly, I suppose,' she said. 'You will do what you have to do while I go shopping.'

'I fear I shall have an extravagant wife,' was his teasing rejoinder. 'All those fashions, those glamorous dresses you wore for me on that fateful occasion when I looked at you and was lost—though at the time I didn't know it, of course.'

'It's a pity you can't supply me with all my clothes,' said Julie.

'No, I deal with wholesalers, as you are aware. But in any case, a girl likes to go round the fashion boutiques and choose exactly what suits her.'

'You're so nice to me, Chris.' They were standing close, holding hands by the empty fireplace, and Chris murmured softly,

'How about your being nice to me, my love . . . ?'

She gave a shaky little laugh and snuggled close to his chest, delighting in the feel of silk over the wiry hairs beneath.

'You're sexy,' she told him, lifting a hand to caress his nape.

'And what about you?' came the instant challenge. 'You are doing all the tempting—shameless hussy!'

Again she laughed.

'Shall we have a drink?' she teased, lifting dancing eyes to his.

He gave her a little shake.

'No, we shall not,' he answered firmly. 'We can find something far more congenial to do!'

'Congenial?' she protested. 'Can't you find anything more romantic than a word like that?'

He had to laugh, then swung her right off her feet and strode to the door. He elbowed the light switch and it was by moonlight that he found his way to the bedroom.

Ten minutes later they were close, warm naked bodies melted, hands active, lips locked together.

And a long time later, when the volcanic heat had cooled and they lay close to the quiet aftermath of the flight to paradise, Chris murmured fervently, 'Don't ever let it be any different from this, my love.'

'No . . .' Julie was already on the brink of sleep. 'No . . . darling . . .'

It was not until she actually saw the two girls that Julie realised just how tense she had been from the moment of waking.

'We did it!' from Androula as if she had performed a feat no less spectacular than climbing Everest. Julie had to laugh, her eyes on Sophia's grave little face, a faintly troubled face which brought the anxious enquiry, 'All went well, Sophia? Nothing's the matter?'

The girl managed a trembling little laugh.

'I'm just a little bit scared,' she admitted. 'It is such a great big step, you know.'

Julie nodded understandingly.

'But it will be worth all the anxiety and fear. I think you are two very brave young ladies.'

'I felt wonderful the moment I was on the aeroplane,' confessed Androula, whose face was animated, whose eyes were brighter than Julie had seen them before. 'It was as if the—shackles—is that the right word?' And when Julie nodded she went on, 'As if the shackles had been taken off and I wanted to fly away into the big blue sky!'

'Which is exactly what you did,' returned Julie laughingly as she picked up one heavy suitcase and a smaller flight bag. 'Come on, I have a taxi waiting.'

'You managed to leave the office early, then?'

'I'll tell you all about it as we drive to the apartment.'

'I'm in a daze!'

'But it is a happy feeling?' Julie slid a glance towards Sophia and was relieved to notice the strain had gone from her face. She was pretty, with raven hair and big dark eyes. Her figure was slim, and she dressed with care and good taste. Julie thought the girl would become more of a companion to Androula than a servant.

'Oh, yes! It is the happiest feeling I have ever known!'

Julie recalled Chris's words and said swiftly, 'You must always be aware that you are no longer under your father's protection, Androula. Don't ever let me down by doing anything which would make me regret having helped you.' As she saw the bewildered expression on her face Julie went on to explain that for anyone as inexperienced as she there would be temptations, even traps. 'Just take things easy,' she went on to advise. 'I'll see you as much as I can, and once I've plucked up enough courage to tell Chris I helped you then we shall both visit you, often, I hope.'

'How good you are, Julie, I wish Christos would marry you—but he never will.'

To that Julie made no response. In any case, they had reached the taxi and the driver was dealing with the baggage, of which there was a great deal.

Once in the apartment Androula glanced all around and exclaimed, 'This is beautiful! How did you find it for me so quickly?'

'It belongs to a couple who are to be in England for about six months. I took it for three because you might not have been totally satisfied with it. In any case,' Julie added as Sophia went away to look at the bedrooms, 'you can't have it permanently because they'll be back. Once you are settled and have found your feet you'll begin looking round for a place to buy.'

'You mean, I shall own my own home?' Androula's eyes were alive, and it struck Julie that if some nice, genuine young man came along quite soon it would be the best thing that could happen for the girl.

Sophia came back enthusing about the bedrooms, each with its own bathroom

'I'm so lucky!' she cried. 'Androula, come and see! I can't believe I'm to have my own bathroom.'

Julie looked from one to the other and smiled as she watched Sophia dancing away ahead of her mistress to show her the bedrooms. When they came back Sophia immediately took the suitcases away to unpack.

'You have a treasure there,' commented Julie and Androula nodded in agreement.

'I think I might have taken fright if it hadn't been for Sophia.'

'How do you feel now?' Julie glanced at the wall clock and realised she would have to be leaving in about an hour's time. 'You must feel strange, and perhaps a bit like a fish out of water, but given a week you'll be feeling great.'

'I know it—maybe before a week!'

Julie laughed and was happy with this day's work in spite of the confession she had to make to her husband-to-be.

'Let me show you the kitchen, and the pretty little dinette.'

'My own kitchen! I can cook, you know, Julie. I learned at school But father said it was not the thing for his daughter to be in the kitchen. Now I can please myself. Oh, it is going to be wonderful!' She fairly danced around, touching a gleaming pan, a bunch of wax vegetables hanging from the ceiling, the glassy top of the cooker. 'Will you come to my first dinner party?'

'You're having a party?'

'To celebrate my freedom.'

'I shall love to be your guest.'

'The best of them all—' She stopped and looked a trifle sad. Reading her thoughts Julie suggested that Androula make a cup of tea.

'Of course.' Androula brightened as she picked up the kettle. 'What shall we talk about now?'

'You first, and then me.'

'I did so want you to marry Christos but—'

219

'The tea, Androula. I haven't much time.'

'For my first guest . . . my very good friend.'

When it was made the two girls sat down in the dinette opposite to one another. Julie said after a small silence,

'I am going to marry Chris . . .' She tailed off as Androula's eyes widened and her cup stopped half way to her mouth. 'But first,' continued Julie with a broad smile, 'you have to break your engagement to him.'

'He—he's asked you to marry him?' There was a puzzled frown between the Greek girl's eyes and she was shaking her head. 'But it isn't possible—'

'I have never been his pillow-friend,' broke in Julie in earnest tones. 'It was a ruse—But do you want to hear the whole story? You are willing to break the engagement, aren't you?'

'Of course I am. I want to marry for love and now I have the chance of meeting someone of my own choice.' She was happy, with no regrets for the broken engagement. 'You were never his—' Her brow puckered in concentration. 'It was a ruse, you say? I do not know this word—' She suddenly brightened. 'I have it now! Isn't Christos sly? Is that the right word?'

'I expect so,' laughed Julie. 'He knew what was best for you both, knew there would be no happiness in a marriage which had been arranged and was being forced on you by your father. So he asked me to pose as his pillow-friend.' She paused, deciding not to take Androula into her confidence to the extent of a confession that although they had not begun as lovers, she and Chris were lovers now. There was no necessity for that, so she merely added, 'He can't announce our engagement until you have given him his freedom.'

'Which I shall do tomorrow! I want to be the first to wish you both much, much happiness—tons of it!'

Julie looked at her, staggered at the way the girl was already coming out of herself. Free of repression, she would blossom in no time at all, and Julie could see a happy, vivacious young lady emerging before very long.

'I haven't told Chris I'm helping you to escape—' That was not the word she would have used had she thought, but Androula saw nothing wrong in it as she replied,

'Then you tell him tonight, and say he is

free and that I shall come to see him tomorrow—and tell him I want to be a bridesmaid!'

'Wait to see if your father has left,' advised Julie. 'I feel he'll get this evening's plane back to Cos, but we can't be absolutely sure, so wait until I phone you.'

'Are you scared of telling Chris?' asked Androula.

'A little,' admitted Julie. 'He'll be angry with me at first.'

'For helping me to get free?' Androula thought about it. 'He has never been like most Greek men—domineering and feeling women should be servile and subjugated. So I think, Julie, that he will say you were very clever and brave to help me as you have done.'

'I hope you're right,' was Julie's heartfelt response as she rose to clear away the tea things.

'Let me do that,' begged Androula. 'I want to be a housewife.'

'What are you going to do this evening? I've stocked the fridge and you'll find all the dry stuff like flour and sugar and the rest in the cupboard over the sink.'

'Thank you. I must settle up with you—'

'Another time,' interrupted Julie, glancing again at the clock. 'I really must be going. Have a nice dinner. You can have chicken or chops or steak.'

'I'll have a look.' Androula paused a moment. 'Julie, do you suppose it would be all right if Sophia and I went out for a meal?'

Julie shook her head emphatically.

'Not just yet, Androula. I think you should be content with going out in the daytime for the present.' She was conscious of increased heartbeats at the idea of the two raw, inexperienced girls going off alone to a restaurant. 'Let me talk to Chris and get his advice.'

'All right,' cheerfully. 'I shall enjoy cooking anyway. And Sophia can peel the potatoes and do all the other jobs.'

Julie arrived back at the apartment empty-handed, and Chris with raised brows said in some amusement, 'So you've spent all those hours looking for a dress and there isn't one in the whole of Athens to suit your taste.'

'No. As a matter of fact . . .' All the way home in the taxi she had rehearsed what she would say. But now the idea of a confession terrified her, because she was recalling that expression on Chris's face as fury against Mark had risen within him. Julie had no wish to see that kind of anger directed against her. And surely it was too soon to confess, she excused her hesitancy. Chris might just phone Petros and advise him to go to the apartment and collect his daughter.

'As a matter of fact—what?' Chris's query broke her reverie and she searched for something to say in reply.

'I didn't look seriously—'

'No, why?' Was he staring at her curiously or was she imagining things?

'The shops were so interesting I found myself just—er—wandering about with nothing more serious in mind than—than window-gazing.'

'Why the hesitation, Julie?' He put a finger beneath her chin to make her meet his searching gaze. 'I sense a mystery.'

Too darned astute! she thought frowningly as she searched again for something to say which would sound convincing.

'I didn't notice I was hesitating,' she retorted at last, defensively. 'You're imagining things, Chris.' She moved and his hand dropped to his side, but his eyes were narrowed and still probing.

'So you didn't bother to look for what you went out to buy . . .'

'Chris,' she said, moving over to the sofa and sinking into it, 'could I have a drink, please?'

He looked puzzled.

'Are you all right?'

'Fine—but a stiff—I mean, a small drink of brandy would cure this—er—headache.'

He stood staring down at her through narrowed eyes.

'What's wrong? You haven't run into Mark again?'

'Of course not. I expect he's back in England by now.'

'Why do you want a stiff drink? To cure a headache . . . ?'

'I said, a drop of brandy.'

'Julie,' said her fiancé in a very soft voice, 'I asked you what is wrong?'

She heaved a sigh, leaning back as if the support would imbue her with courage, and said all in a rush, 'I haven't been looking for a dress. I've been seeing Androula settled into an apartment. She's left her father and taken Sophia with her.'

'You—!' Chris was speechless for several heart-stopping seconds. Julie never remembered being so frightened in the whole of her life. 'Say that again.'

She swallowed to ease the dryness in her throat.

'I knew you'd be furious, but someone had to help her to get away. She was only marrying you to get free of her overbearing and dictatorial father, so we talked, and I persuaded her to leave home and make a life for herself and—'

'Julie, when are you going to stop for breath?'

She stared at him disbelievingly,

'Aren't you angry with me?' wishing she had the drink she had asked for.

'I haven't had time to think, or to take in what you are trying to say.' He came and stood over her, staring down into her face. 'You've persuaded Androula to take an apartment here, in Athens?'

'It's in Old Phaleron. I got it for her a couple of weeks ago, but she couldn't get away until today—'

'You had this apartment two weeks ago? And you didn't think to mention it to me?' His mouth was compressed, his dark eyes glinting. Julie's lip quivered as she began to explain everything to him.

'I had to help her, Chris. It was a compulsive urge inside me and I had to do it. We phoned each other secretly, and that by itself is a disgrace!' she added defiantly. 'What right has the father of a girl of Androula's age to be so fearsome that she can't even receive a phone call without being terrified of his finding out? I can't help it if you feel I've been deceitful, but when you've had time to think you'll understand the need for secrecy. You'd have gone to her father—'

'I would?' tautly and with a lift of his brows. 'You appear to have taken a lot for granted, reached conclusions that could very well have been wrong—' He was interrupted by the phone ringing and he crossed the room to lift the receiver. Julie watched his face, saw his expression change from anger to interest, and then as he saw her watching him he deliberately drew a mask over his features.

'I see. Well, I have a right to be annoyed—What? Nothing to do with me? We were—I see, we *were* betrothed but we aren't any longer? Thank you, Androula. I'm obliged to you.' His tone was stiff and cold. 'I am *not* piqued! Nevertheless, I ought to have been told what was going on—No, I would not have gone straight to your father. I might even have lent a helping hand.' He was silent, listening for a moment. 'Bridesmaid, eh, instead of bride? I like your turn of phrase, Androula. I am thinking you are already a changed woman.' Chris laughed at something coming over the line and then, 'All right, you have my solemn promise I shan't beat her—You didn't say that? What did you say, then?' He listened again, his eyes alight with amusement now, and Julie breathed a sigh of intense relief. Bless Androula, who must have been so troubled that she felt obliged to phone Chris.

Julie's face was flushed when at last he turned to her after putting the receiver down on its hook.

'You've certainly made a friend. Androula was greatly troubled that I'd be angry with you, so she decided to ring.' He looked curiously at her. 'How on earth have you brought about such a change in such a short time? She has the ring of total confidence in her voice now.'

'Not total, Chris; she's still a little scared by the move she has made.' Julie looked up into his eyes. 'I'm sorry I didn't confide in you, but I was afraid, as Androula was, that you would tell her father, and then it would all have been impossible and she'd have remained a prisoner all her life.'

He said amusedly, reaching down to take

her hand and bring her to her feet, ' "All her life" is a gross exaggeration; however, I do know what you mean.' He shook his head in a gesture of admonishment. 'Trust me in future, Julie. I do ask that of you. I have believed for some time that Androula should break free—in fact I seem to recall mentioning it to you.'

'But you said she had no one to help her.'

'I could not have helped her on my own, but I certainly would have assisted you, simply because I approve.'

'And I've been so scared!' she confessed.

'Still want that stiff drink?' he asked in some amusement, and she replied at once, 'More than ever!'

'You shall have your usual: dry Martini. It's less potent.'

She took it meekly and they stood close, glasses in hand.

'Can we drink to Androula, and hope she will be happy and safe?' asked Julie.

'Certainly it is to her we shall drink. And we must watch over her for a while.'

Julie nodded in agreement, but said after a moment, 'I feel she will be all right in a week or so. The difference already is amazing.'

'True. Even on the phone just now it came through.' Chris bent his head to kiss her lightly on the cheek. 'We now have her father to deal with again.'

'Again . . . How did you get on this afternoon?'

'It wasn't pleasant, and I wish I'd known then that Androula was free to break the engagement. However, Petros will know to-night, because I shall ring him as soon as he gets home. I must phone Mother, too—' He glanced at his watch. 'In fact, I shall do it now.'

'She'll be furious,' said Julie ruefully.

He grinned.

'It won't be anything new,' he returned wryly, then added, 'You'll never be plagued with mother-in-law trouble, that's for sure!'

'It's a bit sad, though,' responded Julie wistfully. 'I'd have liked to have a really affectionate mother-in-law.' She ended on a sigh, then thought she ought not to expect too much.

She had Chris . . .

'I'll go and take a shower while you phone,' she said, and left the room.

Half an hour later she was back, looking pretty in a simple cotton frock and with a matching Alice band holding back her hair.

'You look about sixteen,' Chris flattered, and held out his arms. He too had taken a shower, because his hair was shiny and damp and she caught the smell of after-shave, heady and somehow sensual.

'You didn't say much to your mother,' she observed, and he gave a wry grimace.

'She went crazy almost before I'd finished speaking. Couldn't believe it, and threatened to cut me off without a drachma.'

'I'm a bit sorry for her,' began Julie. 'She'd really set her heart on having Androula for a daughter-in-law, and instead she's going to get me. It's enough to make anyone angry.'

'You funny little girl,' he laughed. 'What is that frown for? Come here while I kiss it away.'

Suiting action to his words, he crushed her to him and for long moments passion reigned before he held her away and murmured ruefully, 'If I don't stop, my love, we shall not make our dinner engagement.'

'Dinner—Are we going out to dinner?'

'Yes; we're invited out—'

'But you should have warned me! I would have had my hair done. And how long have we? I mean, I shall have to change.'

'Oh, I don't think that is necessary,' was his over-casual rejoinder, and Julie looked at him suspiciously, unable to fathom his manner. 'It isn't a formal affair, although it is a celebration of sorts. I feel you will enjoy it very much—mind you, I have no idea what the cooking will be like—'

'Chris, what is this all about?' she broke in impatiently. 'A celebration? Who is celebrating what?'

'Androula tells me she can't wait to have her first dinner-party, as she calls it. We're invited to the celebration of her freedom . . . and our engagement.'

'Androula . . . ? She asked you, when you were on the phone?'

'She just rang through again.' He looked Julie over. 'You'll do very well, since she assures me it is quite informal, but warns me she will be giving more formal parties in the near future.'

'Isn't she the limit!' laughed Julie. 'Who would have believed she had this confidence in her, that she would emerge from her lethargy so quickly?'

'A miracle brought about by you, my clever girl.' Chris paused and suddenly his dark eyes danced. 'I have a brilliant idea, my love. I think I shall let you deal with Petros, as I am sure you will manage him far better than I.'

'Oh, no, you don't! He's all yours.' And

as a mischievous idea came to her, 'How about phoning him from Androula's flat while we're there? Wouldn't it be fitting?'

'Indeed it would,' was his swift agreement. 'We might even get Androula to have a chat with him.'

Julie pursed her lips in doubt.

'Um . . . possibly, but I wouldn't say she's quite up to that yet—though it won't be long, the way she's progressing.'

'By the time she's your bridesmaid she'll be a most confident young lady!'

The prediction was to prove more than correct. Androula almost stole the bride's glory on that sunny day eight months later when Julie and Chris were married in the little church not far from their villa in Cos. Regal and lovely in a long dress of lilac organza, she turned all heads, and it was Angela who said admiringly, 'If she looks like this as a bridesmaid, what will she look like as a bride!' Angela and Elaine had come over to Cos for the wedding, and there had been much amused reminiscing between the three girls over the disparaging things they had said about Chris. Julie had told them the story of Androula, so it was with special interest that they had watched the arrival of the Greek girl, who was escorted by a tall, handsome young man who was obviously wildly in love with her. Androula was plainly happy and confident, and Elaine said admiringly, 'You have a lot to congratulate yourself about, Julie.'

Radiant and feeling she floated on a sunlit cloud whose destination was heaven, Julie laughed and unashamedly said, yes, she was rather pleased about her efforts in that direction.

And after the reception was over and she was alone with Chris she began to say enthusiastically, 'Androula! I know we've watched the transformation taking place, but today—'

'My beautiful bride was the star,' broke in Chris, opening his arms wide. 'You may talk about your achievement to your heart's content some other time, my love, but now—' He beckoned imperiously and she slid into his arms in obedience to the silent command. 'Now, my Julie, I expect your full attention . . . and I mean to have it. Understand?' The voice was one of mock-sternness, and she replied with appropriate meekness belied by the dancing light in her eyes, 'I understand perfectly, my *lord*. What is it you want of me?'

The publishers hope that this
Large Print Book has brought
you pleasurable reading.
Each title is designed to make
the text as easy to see as possible.
G.K. Hall Large Print Books
are available from your library and
your local bookstore. Or, you can
receive information by mail on
upcoming and current Large Print Books
and order directly from the publishers.
Just send your name and address to:

G.K. Hall & Co.
70 Lincoln Street
Boston, Mass. 02111

or call, toll-free:

1-800-343-2806

A note on the text
Large print edition designed by
Pauline Chin.
Composed in 16 pt Plantin
on a Xyvision 300/Linotron 202N
by Marilyn Ann Richards
of G.K. Hall & Co.